REAPER'S RISE

RUTHLESS KINGS MC PREQUEL

K.L. SAVAGE

ISBN: 978-1-952500-01-5

PHOTOGRAPHY BY WANDER AGUIAR PHOTOGRAPY
COVER MODEL: SONNY HENTY
COVER DESIGN: LORI JACKSON DESIGNS
EDITING: MASQUE OF THE RED PEN
FORMATTING: CHAMPAGNE BOOK DESIGN

SECOND EDITION PRINT 2020

To my support system, thanks for pushing me and backing me 110%

SAVAGE

PROLOGUE

Reaper

2012

Being a Ruthless King is for life. Even after death, whenever that may greet us. In this life, death can come sooner rather than later. Not a lot of people are made for this life. We're a special breed. We're a little bit of light with a whole lot of dark.

We do good things too and toe the line of the law. It's toeing the line that gets us in deep. It's toeing the line that makes us say goodbye to a brother and friend. And when that happens, I know they died for the good of the club, but part of me hates it.

I'm the President of the Ruthless Kings, which means I call most of the shots. I determine what needs to be called to a vote. I send my boys on a run to take care of business, and

I'm left with a massive amount of guilt when one of them doesn't come back alive.

Like Hawk.

A brother, father, and a good fucking friend. He was my VP. The one person I trusted in this world, and someone shot him right between the eyes. A quick death, but a death he didn't deserve.

We just arrived back at the clubhouse after the funeral to start the celebratory party for Hawk. It's on the outskirts of the Vegas strip, secluded by the desert, but we're close enough to the main drag since most of our business is in Sin City.

"Coming, Reaper?" Tool asks as he dismounts his Harley, kicking up dust from underneath his boots.

I nod, staring at the busy lights a few miles down the road illuminating the sky. I fucking love Vegas. "Yeah, go ahead. I'll catch up with you later."

Tool gives me an odd look as he shoves a screwdriver behind his ear like it's a cigarette. We all know what it's for, though, and it isn't for carpentry. He's a scary son-of-a-bitch. It's one of the many reasons why I know he'll be my next VP. I hate to think about that right now, but it's just how it is in this world.

Reaching into my cut pocket, I pull out a pack of smokes and place one between my lips. The familiar click of a light has me turning my head, and Knives comes into view. The glow of the flame illuminates his face in the night, and his cold, calculating eyes land on the cigarette between my lips.

"Those things will kill ya, Prez."

I snort, not really giving a fuck what can kill me at this point. "So can a gunshot wound to the head, but you don't see me walking around with a third eye, do you?" I inhale the rancid smoke until my lungs can't expand anymore. My nerves calm, going from a strong magnitude earthquake to a slight tremor. Tilting my head, I blow the cloud of smoke into the air, watching it sway and swirl as it floats higher in the sky. "Anything can kill you," I say, keeping my eyes on the stars above me.

"But why bother killing yourself quicker?" he asks.

I'm really in no mood for a lecture. "Go inside, Knives."

He starts to walk away, but as he steps onto the deck of the old saloon we converted into our clubhouse, he stops, giving me the view of the back of his cut. "We're all going to miss him. He was loyal. It doesn't get better than him." He doesn't turn his head, facing forward to talk to the wall ahead of him. I know the words are meant for me. With that, his boots pound against the old wooden slats, and when he opens the door, loud conversation and music flow out.

The door closes, leaving me in silence again. Fuck.

Just … fuck.

He was too young to go like that. He had his entire life ahead of him. And a kid, damn it. A kid who has to grow up without a father now. I grip the butt of the cigarette between my fingers and rub my temples with my free hand.

When my father decided to hang his cut up a few years ago and make me President, I knew challenges like this were going to be faced. My dad lost men while he was in charge, but it didn't happen so soon into his reign.

What does that say about me?

I take another hit of my smoke and blow it out. "Fuck you, Hawk. You bastard." I swing my leg over my Road King and kick the dirt. "Fuck you!" I scream while flicking the cigarette away. I need to go for a walk. I need to clear my head.

That is until I see his bike sitting on a flatbed truck, all fucking mangled to shit from when his dead body went limp while riding and the beast of a motorcycle skid a hundred yards.

I fold my hands on the steel bed of the tow truck, staring at the metal my friend spent his days and nights perfecting. All for what? I scrub my hands over my face as the door opens, letting out all that damn noise again.

"You alright?" Tool asks, leaning against the truck too.

"I'll be fine."

"What are we going to do with the bike?" he asks. "It's beyond repair."

Fury bubbles my veins, and I grab Tool by his cut and slam his back against the truck. When I speak, spit flies. "No one fucking touches that bike; do you understand me? It'll sit there as long as I want. No one touches it. That's an order."

He holds up his hands in surrender, not attempting to fight me. "You got it. I'll make sure word gets around."

"You do that." I throw him to the side, and he stumbles a bit, but he still doesn't go anywhere. I start to get annoyed. "What is it?"

"People are waiting for you in there. We're going to hang his cut up."

That makes it official.

"There's a lot to talk about, Reaper. There's a lot of loose ends Hawk had that we need to deal with."

My fists clench at my sides. "You don't think I know that? I want five minutes of fucking peace, but you fuckers won't leave me alone. Five minutes. Can you manage?" I know I'm being a dick, but it isn't very often that I lose my best friend. I need a minute to get my head on straight and be the man the club sees me as.

The President. The man who holds all the answers.

Right now, I don't have any. The only thing I feel is an overwhelming amount of anger.

Tool still stands there, keeping his mouth shut. I'm not sure how long we stay outside against the flatbed. It's getting cooler out, the disadvantage of living in the desert.

"Let's go." I push my boot off the tire and pass a few bikes before coming to the clubhouse steps. Each foot I put in front of the other only makes it that much more real. With a deep breath, I exhale and push the saloon doors open with my hands. They creak and swing as they close behind me, and the noise dies down as everyone stops what they are doing to look at me.

Everyone knows how close Hawk and I were. Childhood best friends, soldiers together, and rebels together. Making my way toward the bar, Millie, one of the cut sluts, pours me a shot of whiskey and leaves the bottle. Good girl.

Someone taps my shoulder. It's Poodle, one of the newer Prospects. Hawk kind of took the kid under his wing, and I can tell he's pretty beat up over his death. "Hawk wanted me to give this to you, in case anything happened to him." Poodle holds out an envelope, old by the looks of it. It's stained with dirt and age, but my name is written on the front.

Not my road name, my birth name. It's been a long time since I've seen it. I scratch my thumb over the faded ink. "When did he give this to you?" I ask, emotion clogging my throat. "You haven't been around that long to have this."

"He had it before me. He said he was tired of having it. He didn't want you to have it because he said you'd be pissed."

"Not to interrupt, Prez, but what are we going to do with the kid?" Slingshot is a new prospect who showed up around the same time as Poodle.

"Shut up, Slingshot." I take his shot and down it myself, then slam the glass in front of him.

The smell of smoke, sex, and booze fills the air, and for the first time, I don't want to be around it. I want privacy between me and the last words of my friend. I stomp to my office. The right side of the door is worn where I've kicked it open so many times with my steel-toe boots. So I do it again, and on the other side, I kick it shut in the same spot. I close the blinds and walk around the table to plop in my chair when I see an old coffee mug Hawk left out last week.

Has it been that long since I've been in here?

Tearing the envelope open, I grab the bottle of whiskey on the side of my desk, take a swig, and read.

We both knew the road would come to this. I never would have bothered writing a letter if it wasn't for my son, Jenkins. I'll keep this short and sweet because I don't do it any other way.

I snort when I chuckle. He always loved to get straight to the point.

I don't want my kid in the foster system. He knows the club. Don't deny him that. I want him to have my cut one day. My bike too. And if that bike is beyond repair and that's why I'm dead, fix it. I want him to have it. I want him to have everything. There's a bank account in his name. All the papers are in my safety deposit box. In the event of my death, you're his guardian, Reap. I know you never wanted kids, but man, this is my flesh and blood, and I need you to do this for me. That kid deserves a shot at life. Being from a whore and a man like me, I thought he didn't have a chance, but man, is he smart. Losing me and the club will be too much for him. You're his family.

We've had good times. I'm sorry to see them end. Be good. Raise hell. Keep an eye on Jenkins for me. You were my brother.

I'm not going to say I love you.

Hawk

I lean back in my chair and toss the letter on my desk, thinking about what Hawk wants from me. So many things will change if I do this. My entire life will revolve around someone that I have no clue how to take care of. Being an uncle is one thing, but being a dad? I don't know the first thing about a ten-year-old boy.

In the grand scheme of things, I'm not a good man. I've done horrible things. Good things too, but I'm more off balance than I am centered, and a kid needs balance.

But I can't let Hawk down.

So what the hell am I going to do with a kid?

CHAPTER ONE

Reaper

2012

Three Months Later

"Yeah?" I answer the phone, putting everyone's names in the planner for tonight's private game. Gambling, while it's frowned upon, is a good way to make money, especially underground where people play the big stacks of cash.

It's one of the many cookie jars we have our hands in.

"This is Principal—"

I get up from my chair so fast, the force causes it to fly against the wall. "What the hell did he do this time?" I growl and pinch the bridge of my nose. This damn kid is going to put me into my grave early.

"He set the trash can in my office on fire, Mr. … Uh, Reaper."

That's the third trash can this week.

"He is suspended from school for two days."

I slam my fist against the counter and hold my phone from my ear. That little shit. I swear when I see him, I'm going to snap all his fingers so he can't light another match. I have no idea what to tell this clown who's calling me. The principal knows that Jenkins is affiliated with the Ruthless Kings. I can hear the fear in his voice every time he calls.

"I'll have one of my men come and pick him up." I think of a punishment I can give him, something he hates more than anything. Being ten-years-old, he hates everything but a screen in front of his face.

A screen. That's it. I'll just take away all his screens. That means taking away the screen from everyone else too, but I have to do what I have to do. This kid is my responsibility. It's up to me to make sure he grows up with a good head on his shoulders.

"There is a long list of names here that can pick him up. Will it be, um—" He clears his throat and I can't help but smile, imagining him loosening his tie because he is sweating bullets. "Bullseye, Tool, Knives?"

"Not sure. You'll know when they get there," I say, and a knock at the door interrupts me. It's Poodle. I lift a hand, telling him to wait. "I'll send someone now." I hang up the phone and toss it on the desk, and stretch, then wave him in. Prospects aren't allowed in without permission.

"Problems with the little one?" Poodle asks as he takes the chair in front of me. I'm thinking in a few months, we'll patch him in. Maybe sooner, if I can get this kid to obey.

It hasn't been easy with Jenkins the last three months. He's lashed out and has told every single member of the club that he hates them. He's disrespectful, but I need to remember his dad just died, so he has a right to his emotions. When I was his age, my dad would slap the shit out of me if I acted the way this kid does, but I ain't about to lay my hand on someone younger and smaller than me. There are other ways to make him listen, I just need to figure it out.

"He set another trash can on fire."

"Little pyro, that one." Poodle snickers.

"It's funny until he burns something down, like an entire building." I sigh. "Good thing you're here, Prospect. I need you to go pick up the kid."

"Again?" he groans.

"As many times as I fucking tell you to. Now go."

Whatever he wants to ask me can wait until later. Right now, I need my nephew here so I can talk to him about school and how important it is that he makes something out of himself. If he ever wants to be a part of this club, he has got to be useful.

We do illegal things sometimes, like forging documents and making new identifications for people when they need out of a bad situation, but I'm trying to get us on a narrower straighter path. I want people to know that the city of Vegas is protected by the Ruthless Kings. I want my men to have good careers outside the club. I've seen too many chapters get torn apart by the law, and I refuse to let that happen to mine.

A few members are scattered in the police department, fire houses, casinos as bartenders, blackjack dealers; anything this town can dream up, we're part of it.

Even the cut sluts have jobs other than servicing us. Most of them are showgirls, and a few here and there are strippers. When they work, we always make sure they're protected. We care about our girls. The clubhouse wouldn't have the same charm without a little femininity to challenge the men.

There's no judgment here. We all have to do what we have to do to live.

And while our girls work, we always make sure they are protected. We care about them.

But I won't have my men challenged by a ten-year-old who can barely piss straight.

"Poodle?"

"Yeah?" He pokes his head inside the door.

"Send me Tool."

"You got it, Prez." And he disappears again.

While waiting for Tool, I open the drawer and pull out a picture of myself with Hawk. Man, we were fresh in the gills in this photo, just learning how to ride a bike. We look badass in our prospect cuts, arms crossed over our chests and cocky sneers on both of our faces. Jesus, how times change.

"You bellowed?" Tool's deep voice has me slamming the drawer shut.

"How's the repair on Hawk's bike going?" I ask.

"I thought you said it wasn't a priority?" Tool lifts a

brow as he wipes his greasy hands on a dirty rag he keeps in his back pocket. "I haven't even started it. I have plenty of time to fix the bike before that kid is eighteen."

"I want to show him what he can have of his father's. Maybe it will help get his head on straight."

"Nothing but time is gonna help that kid, Reaper. You haven't lost your parents, so you don't know. Sure, he has all of us, but we're nothing to him right now. You need to give him a chance to adjust to life without Hawk around." Tool takes the screwdriver from where he's tucked it behind his ear and uses the sharp point to remove the dirt out from under his fingernails.

"I've given him time."

"Three months isn't enough time to get over a dog dying." Tool stands and stretches, showing the large scar on his abdomen as his shirt lifts.

I know Tool's right, but I have no idea what to do with the kid right now.

"Maybe I'm in over my head," I mutter. "What was I thinking taking him in? I don't know jack shit about kids. I'm not doing a great job so far. He's setting shit on fire in school. I bet he never did that with Hawk."

Tool's eyes glitter with amusement as he turns to leave my office. Before I can continue to spill my guts like a little bitch, he pauses. "Parenting ain't easy. It isn't for everyone, but even I know every kid acts out when they lose a parent. Stand by his side. Show him you aren't gonna leave. That's the problem. Everyone he has loved has left him. Unwillingly maybe, but the end result is the same. He wants attention, Reaper, just hang out with him."

"What the hell am I gonna do with a ten-year-old? Braid his hair?"

"What were you doing at ten?" asks Tool.

At ten, I remember fishing with my dad and learning how to shoot a gun.

Huh. Fishing. I can do that. There's a lake not too far from here. Maybe getting away for a bit will be good for the small spitfire. We can pack up and go camping, maybe take a few of the boys with us. Since Jenkins has the next few weeks off from school, he's got nothing but time.

I walk out of my office and pass Pirate, our treasurer.

"I need you to be there tonight, in the private room," I order. "I only trust you with the money. I won't be there."

"You got it, Prez."

One of the cut-sluts comes and sits on his lap, running her finger down his chest, and for the first time my eyes are wide open. This is not the place for a kid. We have club whores in all corners, itching to get a taste of one of the members to get that property patch ol' ladies get. We don't have any ol' ladies in the club yet. I'm not too sure what that says about us as men, but we're all kind of young and have plenty of time to settle down.

Right now, though, Jenkins is about to come through the door, and I don't want him seeing any whore with her skirt up around her waist and a cock driving into her pussy. I put my fingers to my mouth and whistle, getting everyone's attention.

"Anyone who is about to have sex, go do it in another room. Also, none of that shit out here before seven. No drinking either."

"Prez!" Ghost darts up from his seated position, and the club whore on his lap falls to the ground.

"Asshole!" She shoves her skirt down and stomps out the door, but Ghost doesn't give her another look.

I cross my arms, waiting to hear what he has to say. This ought to be good.

"This is an MC. We should be able to do whatever the fuck we want, when we want."

"Well, I have a kid to think of, and right now this is where we stay. You'll deal with it until I say otherwise." I walk toward him, each step closer to what I feel like is sealing a member's fate. "If you don't like it"—I grab him by his cut and throw him against the wall—"I don't mind ripping you of your patches, and you can get the fuck out," I roar, slamming my fist right next to his head, leaving a large dent in the sheetrock. "Actually, that goes for everyone. If anyone has a problem doing this for the next few years, then get out. Hawk's kid is the priority right now. If you can't keep your shit together, then there is the fucking door." I shove Ghost again for good measure and turn my head across the room to see if anyone has the balls to leave. Once a Ruthless King. Always a Ruthless King.

"Sorry, Prez," Ghost mumbles.

I turn back to him. "Now, I don't give a shit what you do behind closed doors, but here, the main space, is off limits. You got it?"

Tool chucks his screwdriver at Ghost, and it thuds against his chest before falling at his feet. "Yeah, you got it, Ghost?"

"Got it." He straightens his cut and stomps toward his room, slamming the door.

Maybe it's not the kid I need to worry about; maybe it's my damn members. They all seem to be pussies right about now.

The saloon doors open, and a small shadow gets casted from the sun, and then a larger shadow appears when Poodle steps behind Jenkins as they enter.

"Jenkins! Hey, kid." Everyone greets and holds out their fists for him to bump.

Damn, he's a miniature version of Hawk. All dirty blond hair and blue eyes with pale skin. He doesn't look anything like his mama.

He bumps everyone's fists, and Tool messes with his hair until Jenkins stops in front of me. "Hi, Uncle Reaper."

Tool snorts at the name, but Uncle Jesse doesn't have the same ring to it.

"Hey, kid. Want to tell me what today was about?" I kneel and tilt his chin up to look at me. "A man always looks in the eye of the person speaking to him."

With watery eyes, he holds his head up and straightens his spine. "No."

Damn it, he's just as stubborn as his dad. I'm so fucked.

CHAPTER TWO

Reaper

Three Days Later

THE DRIVE TO LAKE MEAD IS BEAUTIFUL. THE TWENTY SOME odd miles of desert and rolling hills are the perfect way to enjoy a good bike ride after the shitshow Jenkins pulled at school. The kid stresses me out more than some of the cut-sluts that hang around the clubhouse, dying to fuck any biker just to get that leather. Sometimes they cause a bit of drama, and this little ten-year-old has caused more headaches in the last three months than I know what to do with.

It's hard handling him and club business. I've let Tool take the lead on most things, as new club VP now. I don't really feel like I'm doing my part for the club lately, but I made a promise to my friend to make sure his kid is never alone. I'm a man of my word, and I'll die before I go back on it.

The kid isn't on the back of the bike. He's a little too young for that, so I have a few of the prospects and Jenkins behind me in the Cadillac. I'm not real sure what I'm hoping this trip will bring. I think Jenkins and I need to get to know each other, as men. It's time for him to grow up and realize loss is just a part of life, not the end of it. People may say he is too young, but my dad taught me that long before I was Jenkin's age.

It's life. Bullshitting or sugarcoating isn't going to make him ready for the world, and I know Hawk would agree with me.

I wave my hand to the right before I take the turn to the safe house. We have a few scattered about the area, but this one is my favorite. It's a secluded log cabin, nestled between two hills with a rushing river a few yards ahead of it. It's pretty spacious, three bedrooms and two baths. It's just the right size for a little 'come to Jesus' meeting.

I take it easy on the dirt road, going a bit slower than I need to. I'm not going to mess up my bike because these prospects have yet to fix these damn holes in the road. Poodle needs to get his shit together. The grunt work is for them, not members with rank.

We pull into the driveway, and I shut off my bike and park it. I cross my arms as I wait for the SUV to come to a stop. All I see is Poodle in the driver's seat and Slingshot in the passenger's seat, bickering like they're an old married couple. The kid is in the back, right in the middle, and his face says it all.

He hates being in the vehicle with them.

I chuckle when I think of Hawk and the same expression he had when he was around people he didn't like. A small pang of agony stabs my heart. Damn it, I miss that big goofy motherfucker.

"Prospects! Shut up. Unload the car and get the shit inside. Kid—" I point to Jenkins, who is still inside the car, and crook my finger, telling him to get out. He rolls his eyes at me, and if he were older, I'd knock the shit out of him for doing that.

Poodle and Slingshot shove each other one last time, and Poodle trips over his own feet, almost falling, but he catches himself with his hands then wipes the dust off on his pants. I place my hands on my hips and look toward the sky.

How the hell did I get idiots for prospects?

Jenkins drags his feet as he comes to me. He doesn't want to be here. With his attitude, it's clear he doesn't want to be anywhere. He sulks, constantly. He has a temper all the time. Yes, he's still a child. He doesn't know it's time to lock that shit up, push it to the side, and grow up, but he will. I miss his dad too, but I don't let it compromise my day-to-day life like Jenkins does.

"You know why we're here, kid?" I ask, placing a smoke between my lips.

"'Cause I set the dipshit's trash can on fire?"

"Hey, fucking language!"

"You just cussed! Why can't I?" He stomps his foot, and I inhale then blow out the smoke.

"I'm an adult. I can do whatever the hell I want. You can't cuss because I said so. Now, we're here because of your fire habit, but we're also here for other reasons—to have fun."

"Right. Whatever." He goes to move past me, but my hand flattens against his chest and pushes him back until he's standing in front of me again.

With the cigarette between my fingers, I put one palm on his shoulder and point the other at his face. "Now listen here, I've had enough of your disrespectful attitude. It ends now. Today. No more. Your dad was a good man, and I refuse to be responsible for his son turning into a disrespectful little shit. I won't be taking it easy on you anymore. You get me?"

His eyes well with tears, and as much as it hurts that I made him cry, maybe that's exactly what he needs. "You're not my dad!"

"I know I'm not. I'm not trying to be. Your dad trusted me to take care of you, but you aren't making it easy."

"I hate you," he spits. "I hate you. I hate everyone in this stupid club. I hate the club! It killed my dad. I wish it would have been all of you instead of him, and maybe my life wouldn't be over!" he screams as tears run down his face. His small hands push against my stomach. "You hear me? I hate you." He pushes me again, but I hardly move. "I hate you!"

Poodle and Slingshot start to come forward, but I hold up my hand, stopping them in their tracks. I'm glad Jenkins is saying this. He's letting it all out, something he hasn't done since Hawk died.

"My dad would still be alive if it wasn't for this MC. I hope it burns to the ground, and I hope I'm the one to do it!" he sobs, punching my gut with his tiny fists. It barely feels like anything, since he's so small and has no meat on his bones. I have to teach this kid a lot, like how to ball up his fists properly if he's ever going to hit someone. Right now, he's on the verge of breaking his thumb. "I hate you so much."

He sags against me and wails. Painful sobs. Not the silent kind, but the kind that takes a piece of your soul with you, the kind that really fucking hurts. I wrap my arms around him and pat his shoulder awkwardly, knowing he needs comfort, but not really knowing how to give it.

I'm not an affectionate kind of guy.

Sniffles from my right have me staring at Poodle, who is wiping underneath his eyes. He shrugs his shoulder and turns around; not even Slingshot gives him shit for it. We all feel the pain the kid is feeling. Just because we know how to handle it differently, doesn't make the intensity of it any less.

It's there. It hurts.

But we know how to move on. The kid doesn't.

"That's it. Let it all out." I take another drag of my smoke and pat his shoulder again. Slingshot coughs, the kind of cough that's meant to get attention, and I look over at him. He mouths something about a mug.

"What?" I mouth in return.

"Give the midget a mug," he mouths.

That makes no sense. I have no mugs on me.

He pinches his nose, clearly annoyed that I'm not understanding what he's saying. I flick my cigarette at him, and he stomps on it, points to the kid, and spreads his arm out in a hug.

Oh, give the kid a hug.

I nod a chin-lift at the prospects, telling them to go inside. I kneel on the ground, my knee digging into the dirt and rocks. Jenkins wipes away his tears with the back of his hand, taking a bit of snot too. It's disgusting. Kids are so gross.

"I know," I say, staring into the eyes of his father. "I know, kid." I don't hug. I'm not a hugger. In fact, the closest thing I've ever done in giving anyone a hug is when I'm holding a woman to my chest while I fuck her brains out.

Oh, get a grip, Reaper. It's a hug. How hard can it be?

I grab him by the arms and pull him to my chest. His breath leaves his lungs, and I squeeze. Hugs are tight, right?

"Uncle Reaper." He taps my back. "I can't breathe."

"Shit." I lighten the grip I have around him and pull back. "Sorry, kid. I'm not much of a hugger."

"I can tell." He wipes his nose again. At least he isn't sobbing anymore, which I find to be a win. I must have done something right. "I'm sorry. I didn't mean those things I said." He kicks the rocks with his toes, and I tilt his chin up to make him look at me.

"Yes, you did. Never do that. Never apologize for how you feel. There isn't a day that I haven't thought exactly what you just said. You don't trust us. You do despise us. We have to make the best of it. In time, things will change. Right now, it's hard. And remember what I said about talking to a person. Always look them in the eyes. Okay?"

"Okay," he says in a small voice. "Uncle Reaper?"

"Yeah, kid?"

"I don't despise you. I just really miss my dad." He

drags his feet to the steps of the cabin, and the soles of his shoes scuff against the wood.

The door slams, and I don't move from my kneeling position, letting the sharp edges of the rock dig into my skin. "Me too, kid. Me too."

Time won't change that.

CHAPTER THREE

Reaper

Next Day

IT'S TIME TO GO FISHING. I HAVE THE POLES; AND I HAVE A cooler full of beer and apple juice for the kid. I had my first beer around his age, but I want to at least try to be a better parent than my old man. Poodle and Slingshot follow behind us as we head down to the river. It's the perfect day. It isn't too hot or humid, the sun is bright in the sky, and there isn't a cloud crossing the big blue.

There's a slight breeze that helps keep us cool. The river is calm, and the water is so clear you can see straight through. It's been so long since I've been here, I've forgotten how beautiful nature is.

"Hawk never took you fishing?" I ask the kid, plopping our chairs down right on the bank.

"No, he never had the time. It was always MC business. We did other things, but some things he just didn't have time for. He was still the best dad." His voice breaks when he sits down, and he tilts his head back toward the sky, and I can tell he's trying not to cry.

I pop open the cooler and ignore the stupid prospects. I put a beer in my cup holder and an apple juice in the kid's.

He shrugs and pops the straw through the box.

I don't want his mood to get down. The hiss of the beer opening is music to my ears. I take a swig and then stand up again. "You know how to look for bait?"

"What's bait?"

I groan and scrub my hands over my face. "I have a lot to teach you, kid. Come on."

"What about them?" He points over to the prospects who are now in the water, dunking each other. Poodle has a split lip that's bleeding.

"Hey! You're going to scare all the fish away with that damn noise. Get out. Shut up. Or I swear I'm going to have you clean the shitters—I mean the bathrooms—for an entire week."

Slingshot gets one last splash at Poodle, as he never takes his eyes off me. I swear, Jenkins is more of an adult than these damn prospects.

"Come on, let's go." Jenkins gets up with more enthusiasm than I expected, kicking up a bit of dust with his tennis shoes. "We're gonna need to get you some biker boots, kid."

"Nah." He kicks a rock. "Only boots I want to wear are my dad's."

Fuck. Don't cry. Don't cry. You're a stronger man than that.

"I'm sure he'd love that." I clear the lump in my throat by taking a big ol' swig of beer. Now I have to find his boots to make sure the kid gets them. "Anyway, bait. Let's talk about that because what we catch tonight is dinner."

"No way!" he says in awe, staring at me like I'm a god or some shit.

"Yep. Bait is what we're going to put on the hook to get the fish's attention. It can be worms, crickets, other fish, or bread, but we're going to get worms."

"Where do we get those from?"

We walk a bit of a ways down the river and stop when I see a good shaded area where the dirt is wet and there are plenty of rocks. "Here. Worms like cold, wet places. So we're going to dig a bit and look under these rocks, and we should be able to find some worms. Here." I pull the small container out of my back pocket and place it on the ground. "Put them in here when you find them."

Jenkins gets down on his hands and knees and starts lifting rocks and digging in the dirt. "Cool!" he says as he sticks his fingers in the earth. "Nasty." He lifts up a long earthworm and stares at it like it's the best thing he has ever seen.

"Right?" I'm glad he isn't afraid to get dirty. If only we can get him interested in things like this instead of setting things on fire, maybe I won't feel like such a fuck up of a pseudo-father.

Ten minutes later our container is full of ugly, squirmy, slimy worms, and the kid is covered in dirt. How the hell he got dirt on his face, forehead, hair, and all over his clothes, is beyond me. He looks cute, though, like he's finally having fun for the first time since Hawk died. "Jenkins, you're a mess," Slingshot points out.

"I was useful and dug up worms. What's your excuse?" the kid quips.

"Oh!" Poodle laughs at this.

"You can't talk either," Jenkins says to Poodle.

I slap my knee, cracking up at the kid calling the prospects out. "Man, he got the two of you! Quick, this one." I ruffle his hair.

The prospects look down at their clothes, dripping with water and sand.

"Come on, guys. Let's fish. You know how to bait a hook, kid?"

"No."

I show him real quick, looping the hook in the worm's body until it's secure. Once that's settled, I teach him out to cast his line, pressing his thumb on the button to hold it down and then swinging the rod back. Then I explain that once he flicks it forward to let go of the button, and the line will fly in front of him and into the river.

It takes a few tries and a few huffs of impatience from him, but eventually he gets it, and he's casting like a pro. His line has a bobber on it, so he'll know when a fish grabs it. The bobber will go under.

"Remember, a bite is going to feel like your rod is tugging."

"Ha! I tugged on—"

"Poodle, shut up," I hiss, warning him not to say another word. It's hard to keep the men in line around Jenkins when they're so used to being crude all the damn time. There's a lot I don't know about this kid. Did Hawk have the sex talk with him yet? Does he know that his dick is for more than just taking a piss? I'm not sure, and I feel awkward thinking about it because that means I'll have to deal with it when the time comes. If Poodle doesn't keep his mouth shut, and Jenkins starts asking questions, I'm going to drown Poodle right in this damn river.

"Sorry, Prez." Poodle stares at the ground in shame, and Slingshot scuffs him on the back of the head, shooting me a wink as if he did me a favor.

These prospects are going to be the death of me.

"I have a bite!" Jenkins shouts and stands up in a hurry, putting the rod on his belly as he tries to reel.

I drop my beer and shoot up out of my chair with a big smile on my face. "Alright, kid. You got it! Reel, remember what I said. Pull up, then release and reel. Pull, release, reel. There you go. You're getting it."

"I'm fishing!" he shouts with a large grin. His hand is working overtime as he cranks the handle, trying to reel in the line.

"You are, kid. You're doing it. You need help?" I ask, watching as sweat trickles across his brow and his momentum slows.

"No, I got it. I can do it."

"Yeah, it looks like you can," I say, feeling a bit proud. I'm kind of having a 'dad' moment, even though he isn't my kid. I'm proud of him. He's trying, and he's doing it all by himself.

"Go, Jenkins, go!" Poodle shouts, cheering him on.

"What's happening? What's that funny sound?" Jenkins asks, a bit panicked.

I drop to a knee beside him, the grass wetting my jeans, and stop his hand from reeling. "You don't want to reel when it's making that sound. Let the fish go for a bit, or he will break your line, okay? Once there's slack in the line, start reeling again."

"But I was so close," he pouts, wiping his eyebrows with his arm.

"I know. That's the fun of fishing."

"I got one too!" Slingshot says, but when he reels it in, it's just a stick. "Here, Poodle. Go take this to your dog."

"Fuck you. I don't need this shit. She gets the best stuff. As if I'd ever let Lady chew on a damn piece of wood."

"Oh my god, do you hear yourself? She's a damn dog!" Slingshot throws the stick at Poodle, who then picks it up and starts beating Slingshot with it.

"Ignore them. I'm going to," I mumble.

The kid giggles.

"You need a break? There's no harm in asking for help," I ask again.

"No. I can do it. Let me do it."

"Alright." I back off, lifting my hands in the air.

I reel my line in and place my rod on the ground. I want to make sure I'm able to help and have no distractions if he needs me. Slingshot and Poodle are useless. It's like having a pair of toddlers around, so they won't be able to help.

"Uncle Reaper?" Jenkins groans with impatience. "I'm so tired. My arm hurts."

"I know, kid. You almost have it. Once it's on the bank, I'll show you how to hold it."

That makes him excited. He reels the line in faster and sticks his tongue out across his lips. I'm not sure how long he fights the fish, but another ten minutes has gone by, and he's starting to waver. The fish is losing strength too. I squat by the bank when I see the beautiful color of the trout coming to view.

"You're almost there, Jenkins. Just a few more seconds," I shout over my shoulder.

"I can't do it!" he cries.

"You can. Don't you dare give up. You've come too far," Slingshot says something useful for once.

"I can't feel my arm," he gripes.

"I can almost touch the fish!" I say, reaching as far as I can into the river without falling in. The fish's body wiggles against my fingers, and I try to stretch one more time to grab the mouth when my boot slips, and I fall forward, splashing into the water.

"Uncle Reaper!" I hear shouted behind me.

I play it up worse than it really is. I flop and struggle, getting the fish into my hands as if it's the biggest beast out there. I jump out of the water and hold the fish as it tries to wiggle free. I can hear Jenkins laughter, and it's the only reason why I'm still putting on a show.

I know Poodle and Slingshot have probably already sent a video to other members of the club, and I'll get shit for it, but I don't care. The kid deserves a few good laughs. I get up, finally, exhausted from all the flopping around, and I hold the fish to my chest. It's a good size for his first one. It's about seventeen inches long. A few more of these bad boys and we'll have dinner.

"Look what you caught, kid!" I drag my boots through the mud and shake my head to get the water out of my hair.

"Are you okay?" Jenkins rushes to the edge of the water to meet me.

"Fish kicked your ass, Prez." Slingshot snickers.

"It sure did, but I won in the end. You want to hold him?"

Jenkins reaches out before I can tell him what to do. "Hold the fish like this, okay? Right by the mouth or wrap your hand around the head and tail."

Once the fish is in the kid's hand, he smiles real wide, and that's when I notice that he's a little sunburnt. "It feels funny."

"Those are its scales. We'll fillet him. I'll show you how to do that too."

"Hey, let's get a picture of the two of you. It's Jenkins' first catch."

Slingshot holds up his camera, and Poodle gives us a thumbs-up. Jenkins lifts his fish up, and I put my hand on his shoulder. I'm soaked to the bone, dripping nasty river water, and I smell like fish, but it's the best day I've had in three months.

And by the look on the kid's face, it's been the best he's had too.

CHAPTER FOUR

Reaper

Two Years later

"GOODNIGHT, KID. HAPPY BIRTHDAY. I CAN'T BELIEVE you're twelve. Your dad would be proud of you." I hold onto the door handle and stare at Jenkins. Damn, the older he gets, the more he looks like Hawk. It's unbelievable.

"Thanks for the best birthday ever, Uncle Reaper." He yawns and rolls over. "Love you."

He sure knows how to pull on my heartstrings that I thought were long gone. "Love you too, kid. Get some sleep." I shut off the lights and close the door, taking a minute for myself. Shit, this parenting stuff is hard and exhausting. I'm not sure how Hawk did it and was still able to find time to be in the club.

Music from the main room is muted through the steel door I had installed between the hallway and Jenkins' bedroom, so he doesn't hear all the commotion going on. This place is my home, and it's his home now too, and the members have been good about following my rules. Now that the kid is sleeping, the adults can have a good time.

And fuck do I need a good time.

I need a real fucking good time.

I haven't gotten laid in months because it's just too damn difficult with a kid always around, but that ends tonight. I'm going to grab my favorite cut-slut and take her to my room, which is on the other side of the clubhouse. Thank god.

I walk into the main room, and everyone is there: Slingshot, Tool, Poodle, Pirate, Knives, Bullseye, Ghost, Tank and a few dozen others. Everyone lifts their mugs that are full of beer as I come into view, cheering, shouting, and celebrating that somehow, someway, we were all able to keep this kid alive for the past two years without his father.

Sounds pathetic, but it's something I'm damn proud of, especially with all the shit going on in the MC right now. We've made enemies, dipping our hands in a few casinos. We own half of one, have a few where we run private poker games in the back. We got involved with the Italian Mafia, and now there's a rival MC on the other side of the strip that isn't too happy with our new arrangement and expansion because we took business from them.

Right now, I'm not going to think about that. I'm going to get a beer, grab Millie, and go fuck her until I pass out.

"Prez! Here's to you," Tool shouts, lifting his beer in the air. "To a good Prez, a good uncle, friend, and brother. Here's to more, the many, and the MC!"

"Aye!"

"More the many!"

"More the many!"

"Here, here!"

Darcy, the bartender, grabs me a beer from behind the bar and slides it over to me on the old counter. "Congrats, Prez. Today was a big deal."

"I suppose it was." I take a swig of cheap beer, sighing when the carbonation burns my chest as I swallow. Feels good after a long day like today. We had at least twenty kids from Jenkins' class to come play laser tag. All the members showed up. They had to. I made them, but they all had fun. All these childish assholes played with the kids the entire day. Jenkins has changed the morale of the club. Before him, we were too dangerous, too heartless, and we were getting involved in things we shouldn't have even thought about getting in.

The death of Hawk and the innocence of Jenkins reminded the club of what was important. The members were on board with toeing the line of the law instead of staying crossed it. I don't see myself going back either. Life is good. Too damn good.

Avengers balloons are still blown up all over the place, and the leftover cake is in the middle of a table where the guys are picking at it. A few of the members are in corners with cut-sluts. Tool is now cuddled up with two of them, but Millie is standing all by her lonesome, begging for some company.

After all these years of being with the club, she's still chasing the property patch. I can't say I blame her. If a woman in the club ever becomes an ol' lady, it'll be a big deal. We protect everyone in this club with our lives, and having someone by your side, wearing your patch? Damn, I'd kill to see the day for that to happen to me.

I sit on the stool and wait for her to come to me. I know she will. She does every time. She's dying to be my ol' lady, but cut-sluts are just that—a good fuck. Nothing more, nothing less. Millie is a sweet girl, and maybe one day when she grows bored of being passed around like a cheap whore, she'll realize that for herself and meet someone nice, like a lawyer or some shit.

I don't beat around the bush. I stare at her, telling her silently to come to me. I imagine her green eyes beginning to roll into the back of her head while I drill my cock in and out of her pussy. Hmm, just the thought is making my cock lengthen in my jeans. Her hair is long and shiny, even in the poor lighting of the clubhouse, it shines for all to fucking see.

And to feel. I want to wrap those long strands around my hands while I'm fucking her from behind. I've never been so riled up.

She's wearing one of those tight, cut-off shirts that reveals her abdomen, and ripped shorts that practically fall off her with how little material there is. Her ass is tight and in shape, and her belly ring makes me want to nibble and lick at her flesh. I know for a fact her nipples are pierced too. She blows me a kiss and tosses her hair over her shoulder as she starts her catwalk toward me. Millie doesn't walk; she struts.

She has the most confidence I've ever seen in a chick, as she should. She's badass, smart, and goddamn beautiful. It may just be sex between us, but I wouldn't be surprised if she became someone's ol' lady. She's good like that, but right now, she's looking for one thing.

And I have it.

A grin forms on her pretty plump lips, and she takes my beer from my hand, taking a long swig. My eyes drop to her throat as I watch the flawless column bob. I don't know where I want to look more.

Her glossy lips are around the neck of the bottle, and I imagine it's my cock instead. I watch her swallow and imagine it's my cum.

"Hey, Reaper." Her tongue flicks the top of the bottle. Fucking tease.

"Millie," I growl, turning on my stool so my body is facing hers.

"It's been a long time." Her nails tap against the bar as she bends over, and her shirt falls down, revealing the black outline of her bra pushing up those succulent tits.

"I've been a busy man. I have a kid now, you know."

"I know. You hardly have time for me anymore." She pouts her bottom lip, running that red-painted nail down my chest.

Just the slight touch has my sack pulling tight, and my entire body trembles. My cock leaks like a sieve, pleading with me to end this back and forth flirting and take her to my room.

"I have time for you now. How about we go to my room." I push her hair back, tucking it behind her ear. I bring my lips to the delicate shell, flicking my tongue across the globe. "I'll eat that pretty pink pussy how you like, and then I'll fuck you all night. How does that sound?"

"Depends," she says.

"On what?"

"If I get to suck your cock in the morning."

"Baby, you can suck my cock anytime you want. You never have to ask." I stand up and down the rest of the beer, and the cold temperature makes my eyes burn as it settles in my stomach. I slam the empty bottle on the bar and grab Millie's hand. It's soft in mine, and the anticipation of having those nails digging into my chest as she rides me has me almost running to my room.

"Woo! Get it, Prez!" Poodle shouts, half drunk. Something falls and hits the floor, and with the roar of laughter behind me, I can bet anything his dumbass fell off of whatever chair he was in.

I kick the bedroom door open and toss Millie on the bed. Her tits bounce from the force. I take off my cut and lay it on the chair, then grab my shirt from behind the collar and pull it over my head.

"Damn, Reaper. You sure haven't let yourself go, have you?"

"You know the game here, right, Millie?"

"Nothing has changed, baby," she says, getting up on her knees. She takes her shirt off and tosses it on the floor, then her bra, and her beautiful, ripe tits spill out. My eyes focus on the bars piercing her nipples. My tongue begs for a taste. Stepping forward, I unbutton my pants and kick my jeans off.

My cock stands tall and proud, a little bit angry too since it's been so long. I wrap my hand around my dick and a bead of precum flows out. I rub it into the flesh, using it as lubricant. Millie licks her lips and inches forward.

I yank her head back by her hair and bend down, snarling as I speak, "Not right now. Right now, I want your cunt."

"You said I could suck it when I want," she whines.

"Well, I changed my mind. Take off your shorts and spread your legs."

She leans back and wiggles her ass out of those tiny things she calls shorts. They shouldn't even be called shorts. I grin when I see she isn't wearing panties.

"Good girl, making it easy on me."

"Do I get a reward for being good, Reaper?" She tugs on her nipple rings.

I shoulder my way between her thighs and flatten my tongue on her glistening sheath. Millie cries out when I shove my tongue in her hole, then I pull it out to lap on her bundle of nerves. "What do you think?" I blow cold air on her clit, and Millie trembles.

Fuck. It's been too long since I've tasted pussy. I dive back in, feasting on her like I'm a starving man. Her moans are loud, echoing off the walls. For a second, I worry about the kid, but then I remember the nearly soundproof door I had put in place just for instances like this.

Millie shatters, chanting my name as she comes into mouth, just like I knew she would. She scrapes her fingers across my back, and the sting causes my cock to ooze clear fluid. I kiss my way up her body until I'm at her tits, sucking each one into my mouth. The piercings click against my teeth before I let go. I open the drawer to my nightstand and pull out a condom. I'm not stupid. I always suit up.

And there's one rule I always have: I don't kiss cut-sluts. Never have. Never will. I'll eat pussy, fuck them, have them suck my cock, but kissing is way too intimate. It can lead to feelings and shit I'm not about right now. Millie knows the deal. Her back arches off the bed when I settle between her legs and slap her clit with my cock. She relaxes into the mattress on a breathy sigh.

I lift her legs, all smooth and freshly waxed, and put them on my shoulders. I take one last look at her flushed face before lining my cock with her entrance, groaning when I sink into her greedy pussy in one thrust.

CHAPTER FIVE

Reaper

Next Morning

I WAKE UP WITH A HOT MOUTH AROUND MY COCK AND A HAND cupping my balls. I crack my eye open and see Millie between my legs, and I give her a sleepy smile. Her hair is a mess from our night of fucking, and her mascara is smudged under her eyes, but damn it, if she doesn't look good.

"Good morning to you too," I moan, arching my back when she hollows her cheeks and almost takes all of me to the back of her throat.

"You didn't let me taste you last night. I was dying for you this morning, Reaper."

Part of me wonders if she really means that shit, or if she's blowing smoke up my ass. It's probably smoke. They'll tell us anything they think we want to hear. It sounds good. It feels good. And past the lust and all the bullshit, I know it's a lie, but I go with it anyway.

"If you don't stop, you're going to taste me here in a few seconds," I warn her as my mouth drops open when she sucks the tip between her lips and traces the helmet of my cock with her tongue.

I'm not sure how long it will be before I'm able to feel this again, so instead of coming in her mouth, I reach into the drawer again and grab a condom. She lifts her green eyes to me and smiles, taking my cock out of her mouth with a soft pop. I roll the latex on my shaft and tap my thigh. "Come on. Ride me."

She takes her time straddling me, lifting one leg and then the other over my lap, and then she sinks her warm, used, swollen pussy down my dick. Both of us groan in unison, and her hands fall on my chest as she starts to rock.

She looks like a fucking porn star, grinding against me, but I can't help but feel like something is missing. Having sex with her feels great, but it's the same damn thing, and it's starting to numb me. Not wanting to get inside my head, I wrap my arms around her, flip her over and press her against the wall as I smack her ass and fuck her from behind.

"Yes! Fuck yes, Reaper. Harder. Give it to me," she begs, pushing her ass against me with every thrust I give her.

I hold her head against the wall, not wanting to look at her face. I stare at her ass, watching it move as I pound her pussy relentlessly. She's screaming so loud that I don't hear the door open.

"Is everything okay, Uncle Reaper?" Jenkins voice has

me stopping mid-thrust, and instead of lust pumping my veins, it's pure panic.

Millie screams and covers her breasts.

"Shit! Kid. Fuck! Close the goddamn door!" I grab the sheet on the bed and cover our bodies up with it.

"Sorry! I thought something was wrong with how she was screaming."

A nightmare. A fucking nightmare is what this is.

"Damn it, kid. Shut the door!" I shout at him, seeing the whites of his eyes from the damn things being so round with shock.

Suddenly, Tool is behind Jenkins, yanking him back by the shirt and slamming the door shut.

My erection is gone, along with any lust, passion, and pleasure I felt just seconds ago. Seconds.

"Fuck." Nothing like a kid to interrupt and ruin the damn mood.

"Think he saw us?" Millie asks.

I lay my forehead on her shoulder, knowing for a damn fact he saw us. He probably just saw his first pair of tits, and if he didn't know what sex was before, he was about to learn now. Damn it. Sliding free, I rip the condom off and toss it in the trash, grab my pants off the floor, and throw her mini shorts to her. "Here. Get. I have to go deal with this."

"Sorry, Reaper. I was too loud. I forgot about the kid."

"Don't worry about it." I light a cigarette. "It was fun, babe. Have one of the prospects take you home. I'll see you later." I give her a kiss on the cheek and slap her ass as we head out the door at the same time.

And wouldn't you know Jenkins is there with tears in

his eyes, and Tool is rubbing his head with his eyes pinched closed like he has a headache.

"Millie, was my uncle hurting you?" Jenkins asks, and I bury my face in my hands from the question. I have no idea how to handle this situation. Why doesn't parenting come with a "How-To Guide" for dipshits like me?

Millie handles it like a pro. She kneels on the floor and smiles. "No, he was helping me. Your Uncle Reaper is good at helping people."

"Really?"

"Mmhmm," Millie stands back up and pats his head. "Good luck, Reaper," she whispers in my ear before turning around and rushing away so fast, I swear her heels are on fire.

I blow out a cloud of smoke and stare down at Jenkins. "We need to talk about knocking, kid. Actually, I think we need to have a few talks. Is it too early for beer?"

"For this situation? No. I'll get us some." Tool enters the kitchen first and grabs a few beers and an apple juice for Jenkins.

We're all silent. I steal a glance at Tool, who glances at the kid, and the kid then stares at me. I have no idea where to begin. I bet Hawk is laughing his ass off in the afterlife right now. I take another drag of my cigarette and then wash it down with some beer as I adjust myself on the chair and watch Jenkins drink his juice.

Like nothing is wrong.

I drop my head in my hands and scrub them over my head. Tool kicks my leg. "What the fuck?" I mouth to him, and he slides his gaze over at the kid, silently telling me to get on with it. "I don't know what to say." This is something I've never had to deal with before. I know nothing about kids, especially when it comes to this shit. When I was his age, I was drinking beer and staring at tits in Hustler magazine.

"Jenkins, what do you know about sex?" Tool blurts, casually sipping on his beer.

Jenkins' eyes round, and his cheeks turn a bright red. "Um, not much. Sometimes kids at school talk about it."

"Do you know where babies come from? Do you know anything about what happens when a male and female get together? Or male and male. Or female and female. No judgments here."

Oh, great clarification, Tool.

"Um—I…" he stutters and plays with the straw in his apple juice box. "No."

Just put me out of my misery. He will learn like the rest of us did, stumbling through it with awkward erections and no one to talk to. "Okay, good to know. Tool, we need to run by—"

"Sit down, Prez. Kid, you too. Both of you. How am I the adult here?"

"How am I the adult here?" I mock with a high-pitched mumble.

Tool turns to me, lifting a big, bushy brow, and I can tell he's itching to grab that screwdriver over his ear. "Really? Really, Prez?"

Jenkins laughs, and the tension is broken. I shoot Tool a wink. I know what I'm doing. Not really. It's a complete accident that the kid laughed at that, but I don't want my VP to cut me in my sleep, so I'm going with it.

"Okay, kid. What you saw me and Millie doing, you aren't allowed to do that. Ever. Never. You understand? Unless you're married."

"You aren't married." He casts his narrow, judgmental eyes on me. It's clearly a look he learned from his father because Hawk used to give me the exact same one.

"You want to be better than me." I take a long chug of my beer and wipe my mouth on the back of my hand. "Most of the time people have sex when they love each other. Millie and I let our lust get the best of us, and we shouldn't have."

"What's lust?" he asks.

"Yeah, Prez. What is lust?" Tool leans back in his chair and gives me a wicked grin.

I hate this so much. If Hawk were here, I'd kick his ass and maybe kill him all over again. I'm not made for this. And I'm going to punch Tool in the face later. I'm glad it's him and not Poodle or Slingshot who woke up when the kid did, or this would get way out of hand.

"Lust is an emotion one … uh … feels when they … uh…" I scratch the back of my head, at a loss for words. "When they really, really desire someone."

"What's desire?"

"Yeah, Prez. What's desire?" Tool repeats the same question and places his elbow on the table to hold his head in his hand. "I'm so interested."

"I hate you," I say through clenched teeth. "You're going to get punished for this."

"Fucking worth it," he singsongs on a laugh.

"Okay, screw it. Kid, you're getting to the age where you're about to hit puberty. Okay? Once that happens, you're going to notice things about yourself and whoever you're attracted to, and you're really going to want to do something about it. Sex can be oral too."

"Oral?" He crinkles his nose.

"Right? Gross." Tool shudders. I know for a fact the fucker loves a blow job because Candy was on her knees last night with her mouth full of him.

"One step at a time. Anyway, sex is when your—"

Jenkins throws his head back and laughs. I mean belly-aching laugh. "Oh my god, your faces."

"What?" Tool and I say at the same time.

The kid slaps the table with his hand and the smile on his face shows the little space between his two front teeth. He's going to need braces. A few weapon trades should cover the cost of it.

He points at me. "Your face. I'm sorry. I can't pretend anymore. Dad told me about sex when I was like seven. I really didn't mean to walk in on you and Millie. She sounded like she was dying, but go, Uncle Reaper." The little shit holds up his hand for a high-five.

Tool howls with laughter, and I'm left there stunned.

"You know?"

"Are you kidding? Do you know how many times I walked in on Dad? He sat down and explained everything to me, but your face this morning? I just wanted to see how you'd talk about it. Oh, man. Woo!" He tries to calm down and takes deep breaths. "That was funny."

"You're ground for like … fucking life!" I roar, slamming my beer down so hard foam spews from the top. "And so are you!" I point to Tool.

"What did I do?" he balks.

"You know exactly what you did."

"Uncle Reaper, I'm sorry. It was too good of an opportunity to see how you would react. I do appreciate your effort, though," Jenkins says with a snarky grin.

"Go light something on fire." I wave him off and thud my hand against the table.

"Sweet!" He gets up and runs off, grabbing the lighter from the counter before bolting into the main room.

"I'm a grown man. You can't ground me," Tool scoffs.

"Fuck! Kid! Not the damn beard. Shit!" Slingshot screams.

I groan and I swear, I'm getting chest pains from the stress this kid is causing me. "Stop lighting beards on fire, Jenkins, or so help me, I will make sure you don't see the light of day until you're thirty."

"Sorry!" he shouts, but the maniacal laughter that follows tells me he isn't.

"He's just like his dad," Tool says.

"I'm so fucked. And you're on shitter duty for a month."

"Prez!"

"That will go to show you, won't it?" I get up, snag by beer, and walk into the main room, seeing a bunch of hungover bodies and Slingshot waving his hands on his face. His beard is smoking, and a few embers are leftover, reminding me of a cigarette.

Which sounds fucking good right now.

With how this day is going, I'm going to need an entire pack.

CHAPTER SIX

Reaper

Two Years Later

WHILE THE KID IS AT SCHOOL, IT'S TIME TO GET SHIT done.

"Church in ten," I shout as I walk through the saloon doors and head toward my office to place the stack of cash in the safe. Mr. Cellini paid me this morning for the security detail the Ruthless Kings have been doing for him over the last week. Apparently, there is a bounty on his head for a hefty sum of two million dollars. Mr. Cellini is a damn good client, but I'd be a dumb fuck if I didn't admit that the thought of shooting him myself hasn't crossed my mind.

I keep a few stacks out to pay my men. We do well for ourselves. I also still put away Hawk's earnings. He may not be here, but when the kid is eighteen, I'll give him a good chunk of cash to get his life started. For all I know, he may want to be away from me and this life, and as much as I'll miss him, I won't stop him from getting out if that's what he wants. I'll bet he's counting down the days until he can leave. This life isn't for everyone.

Hell, he saw me just last year with a bullet hole in my shoulder, and he watched as Doc sewed up the wound.

I push the door open to church, where we meet a few times a week to discuss what's going on with the club. I lean against the frame and think about the years that have gone by. Memories play out like ghosts before me, brothers long dead who used to sit at this very table here, like Hawk. Hawk's cut hangs behind the President's chair, a cut I know I'll have to take down when the kid comes of age, if he wants to prospect.

The table is old as fuck, covered with engravings, spit, and bloodstains. There have been many of days where we met after a fight or near-death experience to discuss retaliation against those who dared fuck with the Ruthless Kings. I've bled on this table, my father had, and so had his father before him.

Most of the members now are the living legacies of this very club.

I sit at the head of the table and grab the gavel that's been a part of the MC since it was formed. The first founding member of the MC carved this gavel out of his enemy's bones. It has our emblem engraved in it and a fist at the end where the knee used to be. Damn, I don't know who this was that I hold in my hand when I call meetings to be adjourned, but the guy really was an unlucky son-of-a-bitch.

The patched members start pouring in and take their respective seats. As my VP, Tool takes the seat next to me, and Bullseye takes the other since he is the Sergeant at Arms. I don't say anything as I silently hand out everyone's cut from the security detail. Poodle ruffles the cash and fans it in front of his face.

"That's for the security detail," I say finally, leaning back in my chair and lacing my fingers over my stomach. "Anyone have any updates?"

"Another body was found, teenage girl this time," Slingshot says, and the news makes the mood in the room turn to something dark and sinister.

Last month, the news covered a story about a teenager's body being found on the side of Loneliest Road. We said we would keep an eye on it if it got closer to town, and then we would try to take care of it.

"Right outside the strip." Slingshot continues to carve the arrows for his weapon. It's how he got his name. He blows the dust off the stone and tests to see how sharp the tip is. Clearly unsatisfied, he continues to sharpen it to a finer point.

I slam my fist down on the table while a few of the men grumble in return. No one is happy about this. This doesn't happen in our town. Vegas is ours. We protect it. No one hurts kids. And what scares me most, is one day, I'll get the news that it wasn't just any kid, it was my kid. Jenkins, lying dead on the side of the road.

I fucking refuse to let that happen.

"I don't care what we have to do. We have to figure out who is doing this. Knives? You're friends with the chief of police."

"You could say that." He rolls the blade between his fingers while staring at me.

"Find out everything you can. We'll take this fucker down."

"Atlantic City chapter invited us out again."

I glance over at Pirate who's holding a bottle of rum like he always is, regardless of the time of day.

"You boys are more than welcome to take a trip whenever you want, but after this shit is settled," I tell him.

"You have to come, Prez."

"Did you suddenly forget about Jenkins?"

"Damn kid," Pirate mutters.

I stand up so fast and have my hand wrapped around his throat quicker than he can blink. "What the fuck did you just say about my nephew? What did you say about Hawk's son?" I squeeze his throat a bit harder, watching him choke and gasp for air.

"Tell me," I snarl, spitting in his face. "Why don't you go join the Atlantic chapter if you're so bummed about being a part of this one? I won't have Jenkins feeling like a burden. Anyone else feel that way?"

I keep a tight hold on Pirate's neck and look around the room, meeting each member's gaze.

"No way. I love that kid," Tool says.

Each member nods. I release Pirate's neck and slam his head against the table, busting his nose.

"If I ever hear you talk about my kid like that again, I'll fucking gut you. Do you get that?"

He groans, tilting his head back to try to stop the gush of blood flowing from his nose. "I'm sorry. I didn't mean it like that."

He spits blood onto the table, adding to the collection. I plop back down in my seat, rubbing my fingers between my eyes.

For the most part, we keep pretty good tabs in Vegas and have tightened the leash on criminal activity. Even the police know who runs the show.

"Anything else anyone needs to say?" I demand.

"Mr. Cellini wants more protection. Just got word," Bullseye says, lifting his phone. Usually cell phones aren't allowed in meetings, but I make an exception for him.

"Tell him I want double pay then." I lift a shoulder, uncaring if it's fair or not.

"Moretti has been quiet lately."

My brows raise when I hear Tongue speak. He rarely ever says anything, preferring to lurk in the dark. He's pretty well known for making other people mute. He's the person we go to when we need intel from someone, and half the time, he gets what we need, only to cut their tongues out afterward.

He's sick, but damn, he is useful.

I clear my throat to swallow the shock from hearing his voice. He doesn't look at me. He carves something into the table with his blade.

"I think they're up to no good," he whispers, and the tone sends a chill down my spine. The room drops a few degrees. If one man can make Hell freeze over, it's Tongue. Not a lot scares me, but he does. He creeps me the fuck out. Despite that, I trust him with my life. He is a loyal brother to the MC. "Too quiet. I can go underground. Find out what they're doing."

"Goddamn, Tongue. Can you be any creepier? Your tone is so…."

"What?" he bites, placing his blade against Poodle's neck. "It's what?"

"Is the sound of an angel playing the harp," Poodle sputters, eyes wide with fear.

Tongue curls his lip before removing the knife from Poodle's throat. The young brother scoots closer to Slingshot, and Tongue returns to his previous task, carving into the wood. "They need to be watched."

His icy monotone voice makes me want to agree, but Tool's next comment is smarter than that. He shakes off the impending doom of Tongue's presence. "We don't want the mafia on our bad side."

"They won't even know I'm there. I can be quiet."

"That I don't doubt, brother," I mumble, knowing just how quiet he can be. "I'm going to say no, for now, until something else happens."

"Like another dead body?"

"You think they're behind it?" I lean forward and lock my fingers together on the table. "They would be stupid to turn their backs on us. We fund each other's pockets."

"Maybe they want more money."

"Doesn't explain the bodies. Mob is smarter than that. You're just wanting to cut someone's tongue out," Knives growls.

Tongue is out of his chair and chest to chest with Knives. "Like yours? It would be my pleasure."

I slam the gavel down on the table to try to call them to order. When that doesn't work, I take my gun out of my cut, point it toward the ceiling, and fire. My ears ring for a minute, but it works—they all shut up. Knives shoves Tongue away and fixes his cut. Both of them sit back in their seats, and I rub my temples, wishing like hell they'd all start acting like the grown men they are.

"Okay. We're done here. Bring me information on the bodies next meeting." I slam the gavel down again and sag against the chair, watching each member file out of the room. The only person who stays behind is Tool.

"They're itching for some action. It's been too quiet. Tongue is right."

"I know. I know. Quiet can be a good thing too. It doesn't have to be bad. Maybe everything is running smoothly."

Tool taps his screwdriver on the table. "I know you don't believe that."

Something in my gut tells me things are about to blow up. Silence is never good when you're in our line of work.

"Fuck, I know," I groan. "I want you to run the strip. Put your ears to the ground, see what you can find out. Take Tongue with you. I'm afraid if he doesn't get out soon, he'll hurt someone here. You seem to be the only one he doesn't get pissed at."

Tool snorts in disbelief. "We have a common ground, remember?" He spins the Phillips head in his hand before placing it behind his ear for safekeeping.

"Right. A bunch of psychopaths is what I have in my club."

"You love it."

I do. It gets shit done, but I'll never admit that. I slide my phone out of my pocket when it vibrates against my chest. "Damn it. It's the school. I swear if this kid is lighting something on fire again, so help me…"

"Slingshot's beard still hasn't grown back the same."

I chuckle. It's a bit patchy now. The big brute hates it. His beard was his treasure.

"What did Jenkins do now, Principal?" I ask right as I answer the phone. I clench my fist and hit it against my head when the annoying man rambles on the other line. "He blew up another boy's locker. There had to be a good reason."

Tool gets up from his chair, laughing on the way out, saying something about that kid being too much.

"Well, yeah. I always believe there's a good reason for doing things like that, Principal." My eyes narrow. "Of course, I believe that. You do know what I am, don't you?" Blah, blah, blah. "Yes, I'm on my way. I got it," I sneer at him before hanging up. Jenkins doesn't usually do things that big. So if he did, I firmly believe he did it for a reason.

He's suspended for five days.

I'm mad, but I need to keep my temper in check until I figure out what's going on.

CHAPTER SEVEN

Reaper

Four Years Later

NEVER FIGURED OUT WHO WAS LEAVING THE BODIES ALL those years ago. It still happens now, just not as frequently. The teens are usually almost always clothed, beaten, and have the same mark around their necks.

That's all we know.

It's driving me crazy, but I have to put it out of my mind because the kid's birthday is tomorrow. He's going to be eighteen; a man, an adult.

Fuck if I don't feel like a weight has been lifted off my chest.

I kept him alive long enough to be a legal adult. I need to get drunk and fuck. Ever since he caught me and Millie all those years ago, I've never had sex in the clubhouse again.

That's going to change. He's a man now. I can do whatever the fuck I want.

"We have a problem, Prez."

"No, don't go telling me that before the kid's birthday. What did he do?" I ask, taking off my reading glasses. Only Tool knows about them. It's hard to read fine fucking print sometimes. Makes me feel like an old man too. I haven't even hit forty yet. I'm just a seasoned buck.

"It has nothing to do with him. He's actually outside with the rest of the crew," Tool says.

My brows pinch together when I think about what could possibly be going on out there. Jenkins isn't a troublemaker anymore. He has mostly calmed his destructive tendencies these days. He actually made it through his senior year of high school without getting suspended. Feels good, like I didn't actually fuck up all this time, like I did something right.

"Oookay," I draw out. "Want to tell me what's going on first before you throw me to the wolves?"

"There's a girl out there. A young girl. She's asking for the person in charge. She looks banged up pretty bad. Doc is checking her out."

"A teen?"

Tool nods. "Same marks on her neck, Prez. I think we got ourselves someone who survived that fucker's wrath."

Before he can say another word, I'm pushing by him and tossing my readers on the table. My boots pound against the wooden slates, a bit of dust and dirt kicking up a sore reminder that the place needs a good cleaning. I can't think about that right now.

I slam the saloon doors open, and the members part like a wave as I make my way through the crowd. It's a hot fucking day, and sweat is already gripping my neck. A few men are straddling their bikes. Millie is sitting next to the young girl, petting her hair gently as the teen cries.

"Shit," I curse. "What the fuck, guys? Let her in the clubhouse to get out of this heat. What the fuck is wrong with you all? Kid, I taught you better than that. She's just a girl."

"She could be anybody," Jenkins says, standing his ground.

"Boy, she can barely walk. She's bleeding. Doc is out here on his hands and knees, bandaging her up in one-hundred-degree weather, and that's what you have to say to me? Help her into the club, now."

Jenkins must realize his mistake because he runs to the girl and falls to his knees, lifting her into his arms. The girl cries out when Jenkins picks her up, and he has a look on his face that I know all too well.

Guilt.

"Give them room," I grunt, and the members part again. A few of them go inside and get the couch set up and comfortable for her.

The girl has blonde hair, almost white, and I can hardly see a part of her skin that isn't decorated with bruises and cuts. She's young, pretty, and with the way her brown eyes are staring at me, a piece of me breaks inside.

For some reason, I know I have to protect her.

With everything in me. Jenkins lays her down on the couch, being careful with her head as he props it against the green pillow. He is still looking at her with confusion. I know the feeling. Something about her seems so familiar, but I can't quite put my finger on it.

"I'll go get you something to drink. Okay?"

"No!" she cries out, and her fingers wrap around my wrist. "No, don't leave me. Please." Her voice is weak from whatever trauma happened to her throat, and one of her eyes is swollen shut. "Please, don't go."

Her fingers can't even touch as they grip me. Her knuckles are all cut up, and I think one of her fingers is broken because it's crooked.

The coffee table groans when I sit on it. I'm worried it won't be able to handle my weight. I unwrap her hand from my wrist and lay it on the couch. She's too young to touch me. Jenkins sits down next to me, and the table groans again.

"This table isn't big enough for the both of us," I grumble.

"Yeah, I'm going to go. I need to go," Jenkins stands again, staring at the girl again once more before bolting out the front door.

"Tool? Follow him."

"You got it, Prez."

Staring at the young girl, who can't be more than sixteen, her one good eye darts around to all the faces of the strange men surrounding her, and the eye that is open is wide and full of fear. Tears stream down her cheeks, even managing to leak out of the eye that's swollen shut and black and blue.

"I'm going to have to relieve the pressure on that eye.

It's swelling too much," Doc says. It's good to have him here. He's young, a resident at the nearby hospital and a legacy of the club. Eric is going to be helping the MC a lot.

The girl shakes her head and clutches my hand again. Great. Just what I need. She's locked onto me. I don't know why or how, but I do not need this right now.

The pleading look in her eyes has the voice in the back of my head screaming for the blood of the person who did this to her. Her blonde hair has blood in it, and it's a bit stringy, crusted, and matted in blood like she hasn't showered in a few days.

"Everyone, except Doc and Bullseye, get the fuck out!" I bark.

Dutifully, all the members start heading outside, the sound of their boots pounding against the floor. Once the last of them is gone, Bullseye slams the door and locks it.

"Is that better?" I soften my voice when I talk to her, and Bullseye clears his throat. I ignore him. The girl needs a soft hand right now.

"Thank you," she rasps.

"Shh, it's okay. Don't try to talk. Save your voice."

She nods and another tear leaves her eye as she attempts to blink. The white of her eye is red, but at least it isn't swollen like the other one.

"I know we look like a rough bunch, but we aren't so bad. I promise. We're good guys. We need to know who did this to you and what brought you here, can you do that? After you rest, of course, okay?"

"No, I can talk." Her voice sounds strained, as if it's been through the shredder.

"There's no rush, okay?" Then why did I send everyone away? It's because she's scared, and you want her to be comfortable.

Doc kneels in front of her, blocking my view of this stranger inside my clubhouse. Part of me wants to rip him away from her. She needs protection. She doesn't need men hovering over her.

I grab his cut from the back and move him to the left. "Doc?"

"I need to examine her, or she needs a hospital."

She jolts forward and latches onto my damn hand again. "No! Anything but that. You can examine me." She holds her hand to her throat and swallows. "No hospitals."

"Prez, Bullseye, she's going to need some privacy. Just get dressed in this gown, okay?"

"Why the hell do you need her to undress for you? What the fuck, Doc? She's a minor." I stand over him and grab his cut, slamming him against the wall. "Do injured teens get it up for you?"

"What the fuck?" He slaps my hands away. "I need to make sure she has no broken bones or any damaged organs or…" His eyes slide to her, and they soften. Doc lowers his voice and sighs. "I need to make sure nothing else happened, Prez."

I let go of his cut, and the look on my face must show that I don't understand what he's saying.

"I need to make sure she hasn't been raped," he mutters, rubbing his hands over his face. "It's the hardest part of this fucking job."

"You think so?"

She's too young to have something so awful happen to her.

"I wouldn't be surprised, considering her injuries now. The more people around, the less she is to confide in me, though, so when we leave to give her privacy, I can't have you guys coming back."

"No!" the girl shouts. "Please, they can stay. It's okay." Her voice is a whisper. "I wasn't raped. I swear. I'm not just saying that."

Eric looks at her skeptically and eventually nods. "I still need to check your torso and make sure you don't have any internal bleeding."

"Okay."

"I'll be right outside, okay?" I tell her, not wanting to leave, but knowing I have to. Is this because I'm a father now? I raised Jenkins, and now I have this urge to save every stray that comes in the door?

"Please, don't go."

"Kid..." I sigh, watching Bullseye disappear into the kitchen. "I'll be in the next room."

"Please."

"Prez, can I talk to you for a second?" Doc asks.

We step to the side where the bar is, and he slaps his hand on my shoulder. I'm not a fan of people touching me, but when he leans down, I know whatever he has to say is serious. "She looks at you to protect her. You can't go. Psychologically, you're the one who is going to keep her safe."

"How long will this last, Doc?"

"Until she's healed, and she feels safe, but don't be

surprised if she always needs to be right next to you, all the time."

"Doc, come on. I'm not a fucking babysitter. Jenkins is eighteen tomorrow; my daddy duties are over."

"Sorry, Prez. That's just how it is. Now, come hold her hand while I drain that eye. After we get some meds in her, maybe we can figure out what happened."

My boots scuff against the hardwood, and I bend my knees and sit on the table again. I reach for her hand, letting it hover for a minute before taking it. "Doc has to drain your eye, girl. It's going to hurt."

She squeezes my hand with all her skinny might when Doc places the blade against her skin.

"I'm sorry," he whispers, right as he cuts into her; the blade opens her skin, and the blood beads out.

Not many screams make me wince. I've done my fair share of inflicting pain in my day, but her screams are different. They make my bones ache and my teeth grind. A waterfall of blood flows down her face. If it hurt for her to talk before, there is no way she's going to talk now.

"Okay, we're done, we're done." Doc places a bandage on her face to soak up the blood, and a sheen of sweat covers her neck and chest. "I'm going to give you some painkillers, okay? They'll knock you right out, and whatever you want to tell us can wait until the morning."

"I don't want to stay out here," she groans when Doc pushes an IV in her arm and hooks her up to fluids.

I don't have a room set up for her yet. We have a few spares, but they are empty with a few members moving out and getting their own homes. "You can stay in my room, and I'll sleep on the couch, okay? Until we get a room set up for you."

She fights to stay awake when the medicine starts to take hold of her.

"Okay, Prez," she says with half a grin. Poor kid. Half her face is swollen.

"What's your name?" I'm careful as I lift her into my arms, and Doc follows with the IV bag.

"Sarah," she whispers. "Sarah Richards."

I pause mid-step and look down at her again.

It's impossible. There's no way.

My heart pounds in my chest, and I'm thinking back to all those years ago when Hawk was dipping his cock into anything he could find, but with her face all bruised up, I can't tell if her last name is just a coincidence, or if I'm actually staring at Jenkins' sister. It's impossible. There's no way.

We would have known about her. We would have taken care of her. Hawk wouldn't have let his kid go without a father.

"Sarah, I'm Jesse," I whisper. "Or Reaper."

"Jesse," she mutters right before she passes out.

I'm not sure why I told her my name. A lot of the members don't even know it, but there's something about this girl that makes me more vulnerable than Jenkins did.

Maybe it's because she's a girl. I've always had a soft spot for women. I don't like it when they get hurt, especially like this.

I lay her down on my bed and bring the blanket to her chin, wondering just how much more complicated my life is going to be. I know one thing, I haven't felt blood on my hands in a while, and when she tells me who did this to her, I'm going to make sure he never hurts anyone ever again.

I'll reap his fucking soul.

CHAPTER EIGHT

Sarah

I wake up in a cold sweat, and the shadow of my abuser hovers over me. I can't stop the scream that tears from my throat. My cheeks are wet. The tears won't stop. I taste blood.

The dark. I hate the dark. Why is it so dark?

He'll get me. He always gets me.

"Hey! Hey, shhh, it's okay. You're okay."

"No! Get away from me. Get away! Don't touch me!"

I scream when I hear his voice. He's here. He found me. He always said he would find me.

He grabs my wrist, and my body bends as I try to get away.

"Please, stop. No more. Get away from me," I wail at the top of my lungs, managing to get one arm free and swinging it forward. I can't see anything, but it's with some satisfaction I feel my knuckles land on someone's face.

"Fuck you!" I spit.

"Damn it, Prez!" the man shouts.

Prez? There's someone else here to hurt me.

I swing my arm again, hitting him across the cheeks. My knuckles ache in protest, but I still have fight in me.

I still have some fight.

But I'm getting tired. The constant fighting. The constant nightmare. I can't do it anymore.

Just kill me.

I want to die. Another bruise, another kick to the rib, another broken arm, the pain is just too much.

"Just put me out of my misery, and stop this," I sob, hoping the nightmare is about to stop. What do I need to do? Do I need to beg for him to kill me? I don't understand.

Let my body fall, let it break; let it go.

"What happened?!" A voice that makes my fear diminish booms through the room. The sound brings me peace. It shouldn't. He's here to hurt me, but at least his voice is soothing.

"She started having a nightmare," another man says. "I tried to wake her up to calm her down, but it's a night terror; she's reliving an experience. Waking her is dangerous. I need to sedate her."

Sedation? He's going to abuse me while I'm asleep? "No! Please, don't do any more. I can't handle any more."

I feel so pathetic, pleading for death the way I am.

"Sarah," that deep voice that makes me feel all warm and cozy gets closer, and all I smell is cigarettes and leather.

The bed dips from his weight. It gives me an odd sense of home, something I've never had before. The palm of his hand lands on my chest, and the width and weight of it causes me to take a deep breath, relaxing. "You're safe here. You're safe. You remember the Ruthless Kings MC? You came here. You're safe." The mattress moves again from his weight, and panic claws its way up my throat, thinking the one person who is my safety blanket is leaving me.

He's leaving. He can't go. I feel better when he is here.

The light clicks on, illuminating half his face. He looks at me with dark eyes that exude power. His thick hair is a bit unruly, just like the rest of him. Reaper isn't the kind of man who can be tamed; he's the kind of man who could break me.

I should be afraid of him.

I should try to get away from him.

But for some reason, he cradles me as if I'm a broken bird. Maybe I am. Maybe he will be able to give me back my wings.

"See? It's me. Reaper. You remember me? You're safe here. I'm going to keep you safe. Nothing is ever going to happen to you again."

His knuckles brush against the apples of my cheeks, wiping away the tears. The promise in his eyes tells me I can believe him.

"Reaper," I say his name as if he is a god. "You're here." I reach for his face with my hand, needing to touch him, but right as my palm is about to land on his cheek, he pulls away from me.

The rejection hurts, but I'm not going to give up.

"I'm here, little one. I'm not going anywhere. Doc here was just trying to make sure you were okay." He scoots closer to me, and I can't help but think that is his way of wanting to be near me. I want to reach out to him so bad, but I can't.

I slide my gaze off Reaper and see a man with a split lip, holding a tissue to it to stop the bleeding.

"You have a mean right hook, Sarah," he teases.

I don't find it funny. "Yeah, I've had a lot of practice."

Every day with my foster dad was a battle. Every morning from the time I woke up to the time I went to bed, I was his whipping post. Some days I took the abuse, but other days I fought back.

Those days were his favorite. I knew I shouldn't have given him the satisfaction, but I wanted out so bad. Those days, he kept me in the basement.

I'll never forget the cold cement beneath my hands and knees, or the feeling of the metal collar that chained my neck to the wall. He'd pour me a bowl of water, like I was his bitch, like a damn dog. He'd leave me in the dark for hours, sometimes days.

The sound of his boots against the wooden staircase sounded like a giant looking for his next meal.

Fee. Stomp.

Fi. Stomp.

Fo. Stomp.

Fum. Stomp.

My least favorite sound—the rhythm of a killer, the signal of my lost hope, and the sound of my impending doom.

Reaper growls, yanking me from my wicked thoughts, and grabs my hand. His fingers are so big that one of his is equal to two of mine. He makes me feel things I've never felt before.

"You don't have to fight anymore, okay? Doc here is going to give you some pain meds, and then I'll be in the living room—"

"No!" I sit up, ignoring the pain in my abdomen. Terror makes my heart feel like it might explode. I cling to his hand like my life depends on it. "Please stay with me," I beg. "Please, I only feel safe with you here. Don't leave me again; don't go," I want him to hold me, to wrap his big body around me and use it as a shield from the outside world.

Reaper is my protector.

He sighs, and that dark blond hair falls in his face again, making him seem more menacing than I believe he actually is.

"I don't think that's a good idea." As his fingers rub the back of my hand, I stare at the tattoo on his forearm—a skull biting into a bleeding heart. I feel as though he is biting into me, eating away at what is left of my soul. I want him to have it.

It's intense, but I know it's real. Something like this has to be.

Does that mean he doesn't trust himself with me? Hope flares in my soul that I thought was long gone. He wants me. I want him too. I've loved him from the moment I saw him.

"I'll crash on the floor. No more punching Doc, okay?"

I want him to stay in the bed, but I feel better knowing he's in the same room. None of the other members give me this feeling of security. Only Reaper.

"Okay." I nod and give him a lopsided swollen smile. "Thank you."

"Let Doc give you medicine, okay? You have to. My orders." Reaper stands from the bed and opens his closet. He grabs pillows and blankets from the top shelf, tossing them on the ground right next to the bed.

"Yes, sir," I let slip from my mouth. I don't miss how he pauses as he sits on the floor.

"Go to sleep, little one. I'll be here. Nothing is going to happen to you on my watch."

Doc comes back with a large needle and inserts it in my IV. "You're going to feel loopy in a second. You're okay, alright?"

"I know." I fall back onto the pillow with a drug-induced grin on my face. "Reaper is here."

Everything is going to be okay. I'm going to be fine. I'm alive.

And one day, he is going to love me just as much as I love him.

CHAPTER NINE

Reaper

Next Day

"How is she?" the kid asks, popping a squat in the chair next to me. His eyes fall on my bedroom door, where Sarah is. He knows something. The kid is smart, inquisitive; there is something about her that he recognizes, and it makes my gut churn.

I'm getting too old for shit like this.

"I don't know," I tell him. "We didn't get much out of her yesterday. Doc had to drain the swelling around her eye, and then he gave her some medicine that knocked her out." I omit the fact that I spent the night on the floor in the room with her. I haven't slept a wink, and I'm exhausted.

The way she looked at me yesterday left me feeling unsettled. She's attached to me, and there's something about her that makes me want to attach myself right back to her.

I need to keep my distance. The pleading look in her eyes, her broken soul, the hopelessness pouring off her every time I'm near gets to me. I want to fix it for her. I want to be there for her.

She wanted me to stay in the bed last night. Sarah is dangerous.

Fucking jailbait is what she is.

"She looks familiar, maybe from school or something," he says.

"Yeah, maybe," I say, not entirely convinced.

"I want to hold off on my birthday party," he states suddenly. "I'll be eighteen tomorrow too."

"Why? Everything is all set."

"I don't want it crowded for her. I don't know, Uncle Reaper. Something is telling me.... I just can't put my finger on it, okay?"

"I get it. I'll let everyone know. You still have school. Go," I tell him. "I'll call you if anything changes."

I hope he isn't interested in her. Just in case she is his sister.

Jenkins looks at the door again and tosses his motorcycle keys in the air. When he turned sixteen, I told him if he wanted a bike, he had to get it himself. He basically built the thing from scratch, in the junkyard Tool has behind the garage. It works, but damn it, the bike is a real piece of shit.

He flips his hair over his forehead, looking like he has a twitch in his neck, and he nods before heading out the door. I breathe a sigh of relief when he leaves. I have a good eight hours before I have to worry about him and the connection with her.

"Hey, Prez," Doc says when he enters the room. He looks like shit. His hair is all over the place, and he has blood on his scrubs.

"Did you just get off work? What is that? Thirty hours you haven't slept?"

"Something like that." He stretches and yawns. "I just need some coffee. Have you talked to her?"

"No, not yet. She was still asleep last time I checked." I slipped out of the room in the middle of the night and tried to sleep on this awful couch. I can't feel my ass now, and my neck only turns to the right. I need a chiropractor.

"Where are the guys at?" Doc asks.

"Tool is at the shop, Tongue is with Slingshot, and Poodle, on a run. Bullseye is... I don't know. I'm not a damn keeper."

"The girls?"

"I told them to stay away for now. I don't know much about Sarah, but I don't want to scar her for life, not any more than she already is." I run my hands down my face. The last thing she needs is to see one of the cut-sluts going down on one of the guys. "This is such a nightmare." I run my hands down my face.

"Why? We patch her up, find out the deal, take care of it, and send her on her way."

"If only it was that easy."

"How is it not?" he asks, right as the bedroom door opens, and Sarah hobbles out. Her eye is bandaged, her hair is up in a messy bun, and the bruises look even worse today. She moves slowly, a limp in every step.

"Jesus." I rush over to help her, and she slaps my hand. I stare at it in shock. No one ever tells me no.

"I can do it." She grits her teeth. "I'm not an invalid."

"You shouldn't be walking. I didn't know you had a problem with your leg," Doc says, rushing to her other side.

She cries out when her legs give way. I catch her just in time and bring her to one of the chairs around the table.

"Maybe I am an invalid," she says.

"No shit?" Doc gripes as he pours himself a cup of java. "You shouldn't be up and walking around. You need to rest."

"Can I have some coffee?" Her voice is still weak, and she looks exhausted but hopeful. More than she did yesterday.

She's in one of my Ruthless Kings shirts, the black one with the pinup on the back. It's torn and stained to hell, and she's paired it with my sweatpants that are too big, but she's tied the excess material in a knot at the side of her hip.

Doc steps forward. "I need to change the bandage on your eye and make sure your vision isn't compromised. I also need to check your torso again. Even if—"

"Dude, can I have coffee first before you poke and prod me again? I'm not pissing blood, okay? I ache all over, and I just … give me five minutes of damn peace."

Shit. She is Hawk's kid. For sure.

I get up and walk over to the counter where the coffee pot is. I grab a fresh mug and pour. "Cream? Sugar?"

"Just black."

I walk back over at the same time Doc removes the bandage, and holy shit, her face looks so much better. Her eye is still a little swollen, but it's open, and I can see both eyes. Her face is still black and blue. She goes to grab her throat when she swallows the coffee but thinks better of it. She has handprints on either side of her neck, like someone tried to choke her.

I cross my arms over my chest and wait for her to talk. Doc puts some cream on her wound and then covers the cut up with another bandage. "That'll do until you're done with your coffee."

Her nails tap against the table, and she steals glances at me through her long eyelashes, fluttering like damn butterfly wings. I never thought this would be the place for strays to come, but it seems the saloon has revolving doors.

"How old are you?" I ask. I cross my arms over my chest and wait for her to talk.

"Sixteen."

"Shit," the Doc curses. "Who did this to you?"

Her eyes well with tears again, and her chin trembles. The stretch of her bottom lip makes the cut bleed, and I hand her a napkin.

"I can't tell you. He'll kill me."

"You aren't the first one." I lean forward, most of my weight on my elbows as I try to get my point across.

"I know. The others were—" She zips her mouth shut. "Listen, I saw you guys, okay?" A tear falls down her cheek. "I swear, it was a sign when I looked out my window after a long day of dealing with this abuse, and I noticed your vests."

"Cuts. They're cuts. Not vests," Doc corrects.

"Whatever. Leather vests." Sarah rolls her eyes, still sassy after what happened to her. Good. She'll need that here. "I know those cuts because of this." She reaches into her sweatpants pocket and pulls out a picture. "It's the only thing I have of my birth parents. Are … are they still around?" She stares at the photo with love before sliding it over to me.

I hope she can't see my hands shake as I reach for it because this determines everything. I pick the picture up, and it's a kick to the gut.

There it is. There's Hawk standing next to a cut-slut.

Mandy or Mindi or Molly, or something like that. He's by his motorcycle, the same one in the shop that I'm still working on for Jenkins. He has his arms wrapped around the girl, and he looks happy. I remember this. They dated for a while, but then she just disappeared. No one has heard from her in years.

I rub my eyes, trying to ease that damn burn behind them. Being a parent has made me fucking emotional. It's bullshit. "It's Hawk."

"No fucking shit," Doc gasps, reaching over the table to take the picture out of my hand.

"You know him? You know my dad? Is he okay? Is he here?" The hope in her voice guts me.

I reach for her hand and am careful not to squeeze it too hard. "Sorry, Sarah, but your dad died eight years ago on a run. He didn't know about you, or you wouldn't have had the life you had; I can promise you that."

"He died? I thought…" She covers her face with her hands and sobs. "I thought this place had all the answers."

"Listen to me. You're a legacy. This is your home. You're under our protection now. You were smart to come here," I tell her as Doc gives her the picture back.

"I wonder what Jenkins will say."

I could kill Doc right about now. I give him a look to tell him to shut up, and he shrugs like it's not a big deal.

"Who is Jenkins?" she asks. "Did he know Hawk?"

"Jenkins is the one who carried you in yesterday. He's your brother. Half-brother," I correct myself. "He's eighteen today."

"Wow," she says in a daze. "I have a brother. My dad is dead, and my mom…?"

"Sorry, Sarah. Your mom left the club ages ago. I don't remember her name. That doesn't mean no one else won't know."

She stares at that photo like it's her most prized possession. "I thought he looked familiar."

"Who?" I ask.

"Jenkins. He looks just like our dad. I thought I was seeing double, but I figured I was just imagining things."

My heart breaks for her. Everything she dreamed of, I just crushed. A kid deserves parents, and she have doesn't have anybody. Well, that's not true. She has us. She has Jenkins, and he will protect her with his life.

"I'll tell you all you want to know about Hawk, but we need to know who did this to you."

The news of Hawk having another kid is going to make waves. Good waves, but waves, nevertheless. I'll have to put word out to everyone not to touch her. She'll be one of the only girls here, and some of these guys I wouldn't trust with Poodle's poodle.

"He'll kill me," she whimpers.

"He won't. I'll kill him first."

She gasps, staring at me with horrified eyes. Good. She needs to remember me like this. A monster. "You don't even know me; why would you?"

"You're a kid," I explain. "Not just any kid, but you're my best friend's kid. I'm gonna do what I know your father would have done. He would've taken that bastard's life. He'll keep doing this, Sarah. Who is he?"

She takes another sip of coffee and sniffles, the way she stares at the empty space tells me she's reliving memories she doesn't ever want to think about again. "My foster dad. I've bounced around in the system since I was born."

I know the system isn't reliable, but I'm mad as fuck that none of us knew about her. I won't be forgiving myself for a long time, just like I know Jenkins won't either.

"This guy, he's really abusive, and he has so many foster kids. And when one goes missing, no one asks questions, you know? Just another kid who ran away. No one cares about us. So as his abuse would become worse, he would eventually just get rid of them. No one ever questions the foster parent, thinking we bring the trouble upon ourselves."

"How did you escape?"

"I didn't. He left me for dead on the side of the road," she whispers. "I thought I was a goner, but someone stopped and brought me to the hospital, gave me cash, but I didn't go inside. I called a cab and came here."

"Do you remember where he lives?" I growl, imagining the guy's throat being sliced. I might bring Tongue with me too, and Knives and Tool.

Fuck it. I'm bringing everyone who goes a little mad with a weapon.

"Please don't make me go back. I'll do anything," she cries. "Please. I'll do anything." She falls to the ground and crawls to me, and then she wraps herself around my leg. "I'll go away. Please, I'll do anything," she begs, soaking my pant leg with her tears.

"Woah, hey." I grab her hands and lift her up, trying to be as gentle as I can with her broken body. "First off, don't you dare get on your knees for anyone. Don't ever beg. A Ruthless King, or Queen, never begs. Got it?"

She nods, wiping her face with her hand.

"Second, I'm asking because I'm going there. Your home is here. You never have to go back there. We'll get Linc, our lawyer, to get your paperwork going."

"You're going? You can't! He's dangerous!"

"What kind of club do you think you walked into, Sarah?" Doc asks, scratching his stomach through the material of his bloody scrubs. "We do good, but we do what needs to be done."

She has no idea just how dangerous we really are. I've been waiting for this for years, ever since the bodies started popping up. We kill when we have to, and no one in my city is going to hurt kids.

It makes me sick that Hawk's daughter was almost dead on the side of the road. His fucking daughter!

On my life, brother, I'll protect her with my own.

She'll never be alone again. She has the entire MC behind her, and nothing is more dangerous than a woman with the Ruthless Kings by her side.

CHAPTER TEN

Reaper

"She's asleep," Doc says. "I gave her something that will keep her out for a while."

"What the fuck; you drugged her?" I hiss, stuffing my gun into my holster. Tool is sharpening his screw-driver, which is a thing apparently, and Tongue is sharpening his blades along with Knives.

He deadpans and nods. "Yeah, I did."

"I want to come," Jenkins says from the door. "Whatever you're doing, I want in."

"No. Absolutely not. You'll stay with your—" Shit, this is not how this day is supposed to go. We're supposed to be partying, celebrating his birthday, and I want to see his face light up when he gets his dad's bike after so many years. "Jenkins, you and I need to talk."

"Just say it, whatever it is. They will find out eventually.

Just say it," he says, and the look in his eyes tells me he already knows.

"Kid, let's go somewhere and talk, okay?"

"No. Just fucking say it, Uncle Reap." His eyes are red, and his cheeks are flushed. He knows exactly what I'm about to say. "Go ahead. Say it." The sorrow in his voice tears me to pieces. "Say it!" He takes his arms and shoves everything off the kitchen table. A few plates fall and shatter against the ground, and Tool looks down and takes a step back. Jenkins takes something out of his pocket and slams it on the table.

It's the same picture Sarah had.

I nod my head and place two fingers on the photo and slide it back. This photo looks newer. I think he might have made a copy of it. "She's your sister. Your half-sister," I admit and watch as he takes his wallet out and puts the picture inside it.

"I know. I noticed it the first time I saw her. The picture fell from her pocket, and I grabbed it off the floor before anyone could notice. We look too much alike for it to go unnoticed." Everyone stops what they're doing. If a needle fell to the floor, I'd be able to hear it. Everyone thought this was just revenge for what happened to her and the other teens, the ones who weren't as lucky as her to live.

"Hawk's kid?" Tool asks, grabbing another screwdriver from his stash.

"Yeah," I say, staring at Jenkins. His face turns white as a sheet and he loses his balance, falling against the counter. His hips catch him, and Doc is close enough to react quickly and grabs his arm to keep him from falling face-first to the floor.

"She's my sister? Why didn't… Did Dad know?"

"No, he never would have let her get lost in the foster system."

"You have to let me go," Jenkins says through clenched teeth, squeezing his fists at his sides. "I deserve to be there, more than any of these guys. She's my blood. The only blood I have left, and I could have protected her all this time. I couldn't. I can now." He hits his chest. "I. Can. Now."

"Jenkins, you don't have to do this. It's gonna be messy. It will change you forever."

"I changed forever when my dad died. I changed when I just found out I had a sister who was abused by someone she should've been able to trust because we weren't there for her. God, Dad would let me do this! Damn it!" He slams his fist against the wall, punching a hole right through it. "You're going to let me do this," he heaves.

"Fine, but the emotions? Cut that shit off. They have no place here," I tell him. "Grab your gear." He goes to walk by me, but I grab him by the arm. "You don't have to do this. I've got it. Tool, Knives, Tongue, we have it. The blood doesn't have to be on you."

"Yes, it does." He shrugs his arm from my hand and disappears into his room, slamming the door.

I glance around the room to see all the guys staring at me. Tongue licks his blade, his lip curling in disgust, I guess, when he realizes it isn't sharp enough. He goes back to making sparks fly along the metal.

"Shit. Hawk has a daughter. That's crazy," Tool says, jerking the screwdriver from the dart board.

Bullseye is sitting at the table, grumpy as fuck because I told him to stay behind and protect Sarah.

"I'm not surprised. The fertile fucker never knew how to wrap it. He probably has a hundred other little spawns running around," he chuckles and then gives me a hard stare. "I'm not happy about staying, but I'll protect her with my life."

"No one ever touches her. You hear me? She's sixteen, and if any of the members get too close, cut off their hands and bring them to me, understood? I'm saying this to all of you."

"Jenkins going to be okay, Reap?" Tool asks, staring at Jenkins' door. "He hasn't had it easy."

"No, he hasn't, but I know he's happy and he wants this. The kid doesn't kill tonight, understand me?"

"What if he wants to?" Tongue asks in his quiet hushed voice. "He has every right. It's his blood he's fighting for. I won't stop him from taking what's his, Prez." Tongue picks his teeth with the knife, the sharp end of the blade nearly cutting his gums.

"He's too young for that. I won't take what is left of his innocence. I won't be responsible," I say.

Tool sighs and then throws the screwdriver into the dartboard, right near the bull's eye. "He stopped being innocent the day his dad died, Prez. This is his sister, the person he never knew existed, and now here she is, beaten to a pulp, and you want him to do nothing? Come on, that's not how it works being a Ruthless King. You know that, and he knows that."

I'm not sure why I'm having such a hard time thinking

of Jenkins having to kill someone. Most of the guys have taken a life, but Jenkins… He had nightmares as a kid, and he'd come into my room to sleep. I wouldn't know until I woke up the next morning to find him curled up in a ball on the floor.

How am I supposed to let the same kid get blood on his hands?

"Go outside. Get ready to go. We'll be out there in a minute."

Tool rounds up the guys and heads outside, letting the saloon doors sway in his retreat.

"I'm going to stay here with Sarah in case she wakes up in pain." Doc plops down at the kitchen table and drags a novel from his backpack. It has a shirtless guy on the cover staring into a woman's eyes. It's a romance book. He doesn't even look at me as he opens it. "Don't judge me. Just like I'm not about to judge you. Go on," he shoos me away.

I snort but leave without saying a word and head to Jenkins' room. I knock and open the door at the same time to see him lacing up Hawk's boots on his feet. "Kid?"

"I don't want to talk about it anymore. Just leave it alone, okay? Let me do this."

"I want to give you something real quick, that's all…"

He lifts his head from between his legs and gives me a slight nod of his chin before standing tall. I can tell he's in his head, thinking of everything that's going on. He's thinking of Sarah, of his dad, and of how guilty he must feel.

"C'mon. I had the guys deliver it earlier." I walk out and wait for him to follow.

The night is warmer than usual when I step outside.

The men are on their bikes, and the slight rumble of their engines seems to go carry on for miles across the desert plains. It kind of reminds me of the wild west; except we're on bikes, and we're still outlaws taking matters into our own hands.

Tool throws the keys to me, and I catch them mid-air, placing them right on top of Hawk's bike's black leather seat. Damn, it looks just like it did the day he went down. My bike is right next to it, and I hop on, cranking the engine as I wait for the kid to come outside. His boots scuff against the floor and when he climbs down the porch steps, he doesn't notice his dad's bike at first. He lifts his head and pauses on the last step, staring at the bike that's been waiting on him for the last eight years.

Tool worked his ass off on that bike whenever he had the downtime. It was all but scrap metal eight years ago. The engine is much better than it used to be, and the tires are a bit wider to grip the road better. The fuel tank is a bright yellow, Hawk's favorite color, with a black strip down the middle.

"Happy Birthday, kid," I mumble around the end of my cigarette and blow out a cloud of smoke.

"What.... You remembered!" He hurries down the steps and stops just before he can touch his father's bike. "I thought it was ruined in the accident?"

I can tell by the sound of his voice that he's all choked up. He reaches for the keys that are lying on the seat with trembling hands, and then he runs his palm down the fuel tank.

"Like I'd ever forget your birthday. Shit has been busy,

but I'm not stupid. It was his final wish to give you his bike. We made sure that happened."

It's hard not to get emotional when I see Hawk's son straddling his old man's bike, but I choke it down, not wanting to look like a bitch in front of my guys.

"Thank you. This is the best birthday a man could ask for." He inserts the key and cranks her up, letting her idle for a minute. "What would be the icing on the cake is getting vengeance for my sister."

"Let's roll out then." I motion for us to leave, and six bikes head out on the road.

Having Hawk's bike back on the road, and his son right next to me, it's like my brother is back for one last ride, getting his last taste of blood before his soul can settle.

CHAPTER ELEVEN

Reaper

Later That Night

AFTER ABOUT FIFTEEN MINUTES OF RIDING BACKROAD, WE turn left on a dirt road. Everyone slows down so they don't ruin their bike with the potholes. Eventually, I hold up my fist, telling everyone to stop. My feet hit the ground, and I shut off my bike just as everyone else does. There isn't a house in sight.

"What are we doing?" the kid hisses from behind me. "Why the fuck are we stopping now?"

"You have a lot to learn, kid," I say as I toss my cigarette on the ground, stomping on it with my boot. "We don't want to alert anyone that we are here. For all we know, there are other kids here. That monster is here. We don't want to give ourselves away because of our bikes. Set your bikes to the side. Let's go; we're walking."

I can see Jenkins' fingers twitch from the corner of my eye. He does that when he wants the lighter in his pocket. We follow the long dirt trail, causing dust to cloud from all the boots kicking it up, but we're well hidden by the congestion of trees. The kid's hand reaches for the lighter again, but he stops himself. I'll tackle him to the ground if I have to, so the flicker of the flame doesn't give us away.

I've had to be careful over the years with the kid's fire obsession, which is why he decided to go to school for fire science. If he's going to play with flames, I want him to at least be smart about it.

When we're done with this bastard, I'm going to let Jenkins burn this house to the ground with Sarah's abuser inside.

A house finally comes to view, and my blood boils when I see how fucking quaint it is. It has red shutters with white siding, a wrap-around porch and a swing. It looks so homey. It's the picture-perfect home someone imagines for themselves.

"Make rounds," I whisper.

A few of the guys spread out and vanish into the night. It's hard to believe these big fuckers are so stealthy, but I can't hear one boot to give their location away. I grab the kid by his shirt, pushing him forward. "You want to take the lead?"

He nods, and I ignore the sickening twist in my stomach from what I'm about to let this kid do. I shouldn't allow it, but if one day he wants to be a Ruthless King, he needs to understand what being ruthless really means. Part of me hopes it is too much for him, and he'll decide to go off and be a fucking lawyer or some shit, but I know better. The kid has crazy in his eyes and ruthless blood in his veins.

"I'll be right behind you then, kid."

Jenkins opens the gate to the front of the house, and we step onto the skinny concrete walkway lined with plants and different multicolored flowers. The bushes are trimmed to perfection, and a small sign decorates the yard that says, "Hate has no home here." With a growl, I pluck it from the green grass and snap it in half. I take the pointed edge of the stake with me, tossing the broken sign in the yard.

Gripping the wood until I have splinters embedded into my fingers, I make my way up the steps. All the lights are out, and it doesn't look like anyone is home, but a red car sits in the driveway telling me otherwise. It's around one in the morning; I wouldn't be surprised if the bastard is asleep. He's about to have a rude awakening.

"Any alarms are cut off. We're set," I tell the kid when I receive a message from Tool.

The door squeaks around the hinges, but my rage festers. We have to be patient, but it seems Jenkins can't wait any longer and lets rage get the better of him. He steps back, lifts his leg, and kicks the door open.

"Kid! Fuck!"

Broken wood flies everywhere, and I stomp behind Jenkins through the pristine hardwood floor fucking hallway and head straight for the back rooms. A few of the guys fan out and check the other rooms, but I know for a fact this asshole is sleeping, probably dreaming of his next victim. I stay right behind the kid to have his back.

A bedroom door opens, and an older gentleman

wearing a white robe fills my vision. "What in the world is going on here? Who are you? I'm calling the cops!"

I grin, and the familiar feeling of my heart blackening fills my chest. I throw the stake in my hand right toward the abusive bastard. It pierces the middle of his palm, through-and-through, pinning him to the wall. He screams in agony and tries to pull the stake out. Blood drips down his wrist and arm, pooling on the spotless hardwood floor.

I take the cell phone from his other hand and throw it on the floor, smashing it with my boot. Yanking the stake from his hand, he collapses on the ground, cradling the giant hole in his palm. I bring my knee up and smash it against his face. The guys hang back, allowing me to do my thing. Tongue has a wicked smile on his face.

"Why are you doing this?" the man moans.

"We know what you did," I sneer in his face and yank his head back by the hair. "You're a killer."

"I don't know what you're talking about," he sputters through the blood filling his mouth.

I drag him by his scalp down the hall until we get to the kitchen and throw him in a wooden chair. Tool gets to work and ties him up. I want to rip this man's fucking throat out, but I promised Jenkins that Sarah's vengeance was his to seek. This will change him forever, and he may hate me for it, but if this is what he wants, then this is what he will get.

"Nice place you have here," I say, noticing the fine china in the china cabinet in the corner. Yeah, I know what the fuck a china cabinet is. Shit is expensive. "I'm here for

Sarah, you know, the girl you tried to kill. She lived, by the way, and then she came to us. Her home." I get him ready for Jenkins, nervous to let the kid have the reins.

"I don't know who you are talking about!"

"You're lying," I roar and punch his jaw. "You're a fucking liar. We know because she gave us this address."

"Basement looks like a torture chamber," Knives says, and then he tosses a few videotapes on the table. "It seems he likes to watch the movies he makes."

They're all labeled.

Kenneth.

Maria.

Heather.

Thomas.

Kendall.

It goes on and on until I find the one I'm looking for.

Sarah.

"Jenkins? After you," I take a few deep breaths while the kid steps forward. He doesn't look nervous or scared. He looks like a man who is ready to kill.

"You sick fuck!" He slams the tape in his face. "I'm going to cut you limb by limb, and then I'm going to pull every single one of your teeth out. Then I'm going to have my brother here cut your tongue out, and do you know what I'm going to do after?"

I watch the kid's sanity snap.

The smell of piss fills the air, and Jenkins laughs, a bit mad with bloodlust. "I'm going to shove a stick of dynamite down your fucking throat and watch from the road as you're blown to bits."

Jesus. The kid is manic. I step forward to stop him, but Tongue slaps his hand on my chest and gives me a slight shake of his head.

Sarah's abuser's eyes are round with fear. Jenkins takes one of Knives' proffered blades and cuts into the man's skin like he promised. Names of the people he killed. Those poor kids.

"This is for my poor fucking sister!" Jenkins' voice breaks, and his eyes swim with water, but he doesn't let the tears fall.

"Damn, maybe we should call you Picasso or some shit," Tool says, appreciating Jenkins' handywork.

The kid is impressive, but I hate that I'm thinking about how much of an asset he would be to the club with this mania. A voice in the back of my head tells me to stop him before the kid is too far gone.

Next, Jenkins takes a pair of pliers out, and the man coughs up blood with every tooth pulled. I hum as Jenkins takes his sweet time until this sick fuck is toothless, crying, and begging for his life.

"Please," the abuser sobs with a lisp. Blood and tears drip from his chin in red streaks, and tears run through the dried red liquid on his face. "I'll never hurt another person again."

Jenkins nods and hands me the knife, and I wipe the blade on my jeans before giving it back to Knives. "You're right. I'll make sure of that." He steps back and nods to Tongue and stands right next to me. Tongue's cold eyes are like lasers, nearly glowing through the long tendrils of black hair covering his face. A crooked grin forms on his lips, and when he brings his knife up to the light, it sparkles.

"Are you okay?" I ask the kid. I'm concerned for him. He's covered in blood, but he doesn't seem bothered by it at all.

What did I do?

Jenkins doesn't answer. His eyes are focused on what is happening in front of us. I watch as Tongue takes the serrated metal and slices against the man's tongue, ripping it from his mouth. His pleas for life fall on deaf ears as Tongue does what he does best.

He makes his victim mute.

Tongue tosses the man's appendage on the table, and that's when I notice that Jenkins has turned white as a sheet. He looks like he's about to puke, but he keeps his bile down.

I remember the first time I saw this much blood. I kept shit together until we got back home, and I could puke in privacy. You never want to look weak in front of your men.

"My job isn't finished. My cruelty isn't done," Jenkins says, and I decide right then and there this is too much. He is done.

Tongue steps back, and I look at the man who almost took Jenkins' sister from him. His head lolls to each side. He coughs dark red blood, splattering it all over his face as the wound in his mouth fills his useless throat. He's barely conscious.

"Jenkins…" My warning turns to a sharp inhale when I see that he's holding a grenade. "Where the fuck did you get that?"

The kid ignores me.

"Anyone have tape?" he asks, the darkness inside him

nearly taking over. His soul is turning black, heart is beating, and in his eyes there's nothing but pure joy.

"Here." Slingshot tosses him a roll of duct tape.

If this is how it's going to go down, then I'm going to be supportive.

"Any final words?" I ask the man and then laugh at my own joke. "Of course not. My bad. I forgot. You don't have a tongue."

With a look of pure hate, Jenkins shoves the grenade in his mouth and then quickly places a piece of tape across his lips, leaving the clip dangling. "You'll never hurt anyone again. I'll make sure of that. This is for Sarah."

"Oh, shit!" There are shouts from behind me as the men bolt out of the house to keep from getting blown up.

I'm not going to leave the kid. I refuse.

Jenkins yanks the clip from the man's mouth, and I grab Jenkins, tossing him over my shoulder. I don't care that he's a grown man. All I care about is getting us out the front door and onto the ground.

"What the fuck, Uncle Reaper?" he yells at me. "I had it!"

"I wanted to get you out of there as quick as possible," I say, trying to catch my breath.

Boom.

The windows of the kitchen shatter, and we all duck down to avoid the glass. I cover Jenkins with my body. Glass shards clink to the concrete, and a satisfied smile spreads across Jenkins' face. I roll off him and take in the scene before me. Apparently, Jenkins isn't done yet. He climbs to his feet and takes a stick of dynamite out of his back pocket and flicks his lighter on, watching the sparks ignite and glow. He slings the dynamite at the house, and the night sky lights up with embers of gold and orange.

It's better than any trash can fire, I'll give him that.

"We're gonna want to run now," Jenkins informs me. A few of the guys laugh and stumble as we run to our bikes.

I keep my head turned over my shoulder and watch as the house crumbles to the earth. The after tremors shake the ground under my boots, and adrenaline runs through my veins remembering the sound of the dynamite going off.

"You're sick, fucker!" Tongue hollers, slapping Jenkins on the back.

I stare at Jenkins with pride and concern. He's changed. I can see it in his eyes.

I did what I had to do, right?

Every member does shit like this. I never thought I'd feel this way about Jenkins following in the MC's footsteps. I wanted a different life for him. One that doesn't involve blood. But I know, deep down, this is where the kid belongs.

"How about you lead us home, Boomer?" I give him the nickname I've been thinking of for the last few years and light another cigarette.

The guys cheer at Jenkins' given road name.

The biggest, sickest, cruelest smile takes over Jenkins' face and pride blooms in my chest when I see the strong man he has become.

Blood for blood is our motto, and that's what I just allowed the kid to have. I know Hawk would be proud of Jenkins. The kid—Boomer. I might be a little twisted now, but you have to be when you're a Ruthless King.

CHAPTER TWELVE

Reaper

One Year Later

I'D BE LYING IF I SAID SARAH ISN'T A BEAUTIFUL YOUNG WOMAN. I hate that I'm even noticing, but it's hard not to when she's always around me wearing short shorts and low-cut shirts to show off the small mound of her tits.

She's only seventeen.

She teases me, and it pisses me off. I don't fuck around with minors. Everyone knows the game she's playing with me. Everyone's known ever since the day she came to our club; she's latched onto me in more than one way. It's unhealthy.

And it's driving me crazy.

I'm not going to jail over some little girl with a crush. That's all this is—a crush. I never tell anyone that deep inside, I know better. Once she turns eighteen, a part of me wants to claim her as mine, but what the hell is a girl who is eighteen going to do with a man twenty-one years older than her? That's too big of an age difference. No matter how much I'm going to want her when the time is right, we can never happen. We are in different places in our lives.

"Hey, Jesse," she greets as she sits at the kitchen table, holding a cup of coffee to her chest.

She's wearing my damn shirt again.

"Sarah, what did I tell you about calling me that?" She's the only one who doesn't call me Reaper. "And stop wearing my shit." Because she looks too damn good in it, and I don't need this kind of shit in my life right now.

"But it's comfortable," she pouts, and the collar of my shirt falls down her shoulder, revealing her flawless creamy skin.

"I'm out of here," I growl, throwing my plate in the sink and walking away from the menace. I pass Tool, who's giggling like a fucking schoolgirl at me.

"I think someone has an admirer," he teases as he blows me a kiss.

"Fuck you," I grunt as I walk by him and Poodle and vanish into my room. I lean against the door and take a deep breath. My fingers find the lock on the gold knob and turn it, making sure she can't get in.

Little maniac. She and her brother both got the crazy gene from Hawk. Dealing with the both of them has aged me ten years. I have a protective fatherly instinct toward Jenkins, but Sarah? I'm protective of her in another way; a way I can't put my finger on. A way I know I'm not allowed to feel because she's fucking seventeen.

One more year and this can stop driving me crazy.

"What did you do, Sarah?" Jenkins' voice from behind my door has me turning and placing my ear against the wood. It's a bit muted, but I can see hear it.

"Nothing. He got mad because I accidently wore his shirt."

"You need to stop that shit. I know what you're trying to do. Uncle Reap isn't ever going to touch you. You're way too young. You need to stop with the show."

"I don't know what you're talking about, Jenkins."

She calls everyone by their actual name, never their road name. It drives everyone crazy.

"Sure you don't. He's a grown man, Sarah. I'm not saying this to hurt your feelings, but he wants a grown woman."

"I have one more year until I'm grown."

"That's not what I mean. Jesus, Sarah!" Jenkins hisses at her, and I know she probably cowered from his reaction. That's what she's done ever since she came here, and it kills me. I want to unlock the door and come to her rescue, but that will only make her latch onto me more.

What I need to do is find Millie and take all my frustrations out on her.

Even the thought of doing that makes me tired, though. I'm better off waiting, even if I don't know what I'm waiting for.

Yes, you do. You're waiting until Sarah is legal.

"Fuck!" I roar and grab the half empty bottle of bourbon on my nightstand and take a big swig. I break free from it, take a deep breath, and chug again, trying to drown out those big brown eyes that haunt my fucking dreams.

She knows she gets to me too. I can tell by the way she

looks at me when she does something to catch my attention.

Like fucking breathe.

I scrub my hands over my face and lay on my bed, making the decision to stay away from her. Even once she's eighteen, I'll want her more than the own air in my lungs. She's Hawk's daughter. She's off limits. He'd kick my ass if an old bastard like me went after his only little girl.

She isn't little.

Yes, she is. That's what I need to keep telling myself.

I finish off the bottle and throw it in the trash. It's nearly time for me to hit the hay, anyway. With a slight buzz warming my blood and the image of Sarah fading into the back of my mind, I exhale and allow myself to fall into sleep. Tomorrow is a new day. A new set of rules.

I groan when a pair of hot lips suck on my neck. My cock is rock hard, and my balls pull up tight when a soft hand wraps around my long steel length through my sweatpants.

"Fuck, that feels good," I say to Millie as she bites my jugular. I've never known her to be so forward and rough, but I fucking like it. She's doing everything she never does.

My hands trail down her back and grip her ass, rolling her against my cock. This is exactly what I need.

"Jesse," she moans.

And everything around me stops.

My heart thumps against my chest. I push her off me and turn on the light next to my bed, knowing damn well who I'm going to see. "What the fuck, Sarah!" I hiss, picking up the shirt she just tossed on my chest. I avert my eyes and give it back to her. "Get dressed and get the fuck out."

"You were liking what I was doing," she purrs. "You're still hard. Come on, Jesse, stop fighting this thing between us."

"You're selfish," I say with a shake of my head. "Fucking selfish." I grab her arms and flip her over, bringing my hand down on her ass until she cries out. "I'm not going to jail for you. Get your shit together, Sarah." I spank her again and then put her on her feet. I pull the shirt over her head as tears fall down her cheeks. "Anything jerking my cock is going to feel fucking great. I thought you were Millie."

"What?" She looks like I just slapped her across the face.

"You're too young for me, Sarah. You're seventeen. If you come into my room again and tempt me, I'll kick you out of the clubhouse, and you'll have to find your own place. I'm not playing these games."

"I thought—" Her chin wobbles, and she pushes a strand of her hair behind her ear.

"You thought wrong," I sneer, hating that I'm being so cruel. I long for the day to be able to actually have her in my arms, but not like this; not while she's underage. And after tonight, I wouldn't be surprised if I've pushed her away forever. "You're a little girl. You need to date boys your own age." I soften my voice and grab her shoulders, my cock finally flaccid as she starts to really cry.

Good. That's exactly what needs to happen.

"But I love you," she says. "Jesse—"

"Stop. You think you love me. It's just a crush." I hate

every word that comes out of my mouth. "Don't ever come back in my room." I open the door to usher her out. She doesn't hesitate; she dashes down the hall and disappears. I slam the door and lock it again, dragging my hands down my face.

She has no idea what love is. She's too young.

I've never felt like such a bastard in my entire life, but there is too much at stake for there to ever be anything between us. The reality is, no matter how old that girl is, I need to stay away until the day I die. Loving me will do nothing but destroy her.

I won't be responsible for that.

"Damn it," I curse, and my hand comes up and touches the spot on my neck that she sucked on. It still burns from her touch. My heart still races, and my soul still yearns for the one woman I can't have.

Not just because she's a minor.

Not just because she's my best friend's daughter.

Not just because she's my nephew's sister.

But because I'm Reaper, with countless souls under my belt, and I'm afraid I'll do the exact same thing to her. I can't suck the life out of Sarah when she's only just beginning.

When she's eighteen, thirty, forty, she'll be safely away from me.

And every single fucking day I'll be in agony over her.

She's ruthless.

ALSO BY K.L. SAVAGE

PREQUEL - REAPER'S RISE
BOOK ONE - REAPER
BOOK TWO - BOOMER
BOOK THREE - TOOL
BOOK FOUR - POODLE
BOOK FIVE - SKIRT
BOOK SIX - PIRATE
BOOK SEVEN - DOC
BOOK EIGHT - TONGUE

OTHER BOOKS IN THE RUTHLESS KINGS SERIES
A RUTHLESS HALLOWEEN

RUTHLESS KINGS MC IS NOW ON AUDIBLE.

CLICK HERE TO JOIN RUTHLESS READERS AND GET THE LATEST UPDATES BEFORE ANYONE ELSE. OR VISIT AUTHORKLSAVAGE.COM OR STALK THEM AT THE SITES BELOW.

FACEBOOK | INSTAGRAM | RUTHLESS READERS
AMAZON | TWITTER | BOOKBUB | GOODREADS |
PINTEREST | WEBSITE

FOR UPDATES FROM
K.L. SAVAGE TEXT:
KL SAVAGE
RUTHLESS ROMANCE THAT WILL RIP YOUR HEART OUT.
725-225-0825

Printed in Great Britain
by Amazon